MW01698570

The Dream Analyst AND THE VICTORIAN HOUSE

by
Laraine C. Hall

HP

Hawkeye Publishers

The Dream Analyst and the Victorian House

Library of Congress Control Number: 2017900776

Cover Design by Helen E. Gettner

For more information, address Hawkeye Publishers,
P.O. Box 3098, Camarillo, CA 93011.

Paperback:	978-1-946005-05-2
Hardcover:	978-1-946005-07-6
Ebook:	978-1-946005-08-3

HAWKEYEPUBLISHERS.COM

I dedicate this book to those who have touched my life in some way.

We are all teachers and students for each other, journeying through life. Though we travel different roads, we all seek understanding, respect, love, and acceptance.

—*Laraine*

Dear Andy,

Always believe in your dreams & follow your heart.

With Love,

Laraine

Contents

Chapter 1

The House and the Fisherman

No activity on the beach, just the iridescent waves rolling along the shoreline. A crimson sun lay low on the water, as a soft, cool breeze played with my short, blonde curls, tossing them around the fringes of my face. I stood in white shorts, blouse and bare feet, absorbing the early evening tranquility.

My eyes scanned the beach, up the cliff and across the bluff. I could barely see the other old houses up there, as they faded into the distance. Just one grabbed my attention.

The old Victorian house sat perched on the bluff above the ocean. Like a large white citadel, defying would-be intruders to keep their distance, it was foreboding and cold.

Old…very old, it stood squarely and strongly, large white blocks piled boldly atop each other into a tall tower, like blocks of ice. From the beach, I could see four windows spaced an equal distance from each other across the second floor facade. Jutting out from the roof above them, four windowed gables…dark and eerie, as if the ghosts of its past were imprisoned within.

That's all I could see from the beach, except the gazebo near the bluff. Vines and twigs clung to its faded white essence.

Hanging from the shear cliff were the remains of ancient steps. Once the means to the beach below the house, they now zigzagged down the side of the cliff in broken snags.

Out from the beach below the house was a remnant of dock. It's large creosoted pilings hinted of schooners unloading furniture and supplies for the Victorian houses on the cliff. But now, half gone, it received merely an occasional fisherman.

"You like it, don't you?"

Startled, my heart leaped into my throat. I glanced behind me.

The sunlight had dispersed into purple and magenta particles, and little was discernable, but the dark mass of decrepit dock partially illuminated in the iridescent waves rolling beneath it. Then I saw him... he appeared as a shadow, a hunched-over bit of humanity against an abandoned dock, all molded into one silhouetted sculpture against the magenta sky.

"You like it, don't you?" A husky masculine voice called out over the crashing waves.

I turned and looked at him, a fisherman sat on the dilapidated dock a few feet from me.

"Well?" he demanded. "You like the house, don't you?"

"Why, yes. I do." I cautiously walked toward him.

"It's a gloomy place. But, I imagine most of them were, in those days." He continued looking at his fishing line as he spoke, as if such concentration would compel a fish to leap onto it.

"I suppose so," I agreed. "Have you ever been in it?"

"No, can't say that I have, nor do I have any desire to," he grunted.

"Really? Why?" I walked up to him, thinking he might be able to tell me something about the house. I had seen him fishing here a few times, but this is the first time we had spoken. Standing a short distance from him, I could see he was in his late sixties or early seventies.

"Humph," he grunted. "I'm not interested in old things, like old houses and antiques the way a lot of people are these days."

"Oh," I murmured, thinking he must have a very limited education, and wondering what we would talk about next. I watched him for a moment, as I leaned against the wooden piling, which stood between us. Then I asked, “Do the fish bite this late in the day?” Not realizing, until after I said it, that he wouldn’t have been there if they didn’t.

“Well, they have to eat sometime,” he answered, glancing up at me with a crooked smile.

He had a rugged countenance. A grey beard and thick, white, wavy hair framed a strong, deeply lined face. His hands and face were tanned to a leathery finish. A short-sleeved shirt and faded jeans showed him as neither fat nor skinny. By his size, I imagined him as a dockworker or maybe in construction of some sort.

“How often do you come down here to fish?”

“Whenever I feel like fishing.” He didn’t take his eyes from his line.

I thought, *am I asking stupid questions, or doesn’t this guy want to talk to me?* I decided to try once more, “Does it bother the fish when I talk?”

“No. They’re bothered more by your legs.” He didn’t smile or look at me. So I didn’t know if he was serious or kidding.

“Okay, I’ll just walk on then,” I whispered.

“What are you whispering for?” He looked up at me.

“Well, I don’t want to bother the fish,” I said softly.

“You think they can hear you above the roar of the ocean?” He frowned.

“Oh…I guess not.” I sounded like a silly schoolgirl, but somehow felt compelled to continue with this fugue. “But, if my legs bother them, then I’d better leave.” At the time I was speaking, it didn’t seem so ridiculous. It was his answer that made it sound really ludicrous.

“Don’t worry, it’s only the male fish that are bothered by your legs, and it’s the females that I’m trying to catch.”

I knew enough about fishing to realize he was joking, even before he looked up at me with his cockeyed grin. Feeling very silly now, I laughed. “And it’s this female fish that you caught, right?”

“That’s right, little lady.” He winked with a smile.

Now I saw, with the glow of the sunset, his leathery, old skin had softness, showing a handsome maturity that comes with age. It was obvious that he spent a lot of time in the sun. I wondered what he did professionally.

"Do you live on the beach?" I asked.

"As much as I can."

"How much is that?"

"Enough to suit me."

Oh, no, I thought. *Here we go again. Maybe he doesn't want to tell me. Or maybe he just likes playing games. Maybe I should stop prying. Or maybe I would get better answers if I were more specific.* "Do you have a house on the beach?"

"Yes, about a half a mile toward the sunrise."

Good! Now we're getting somewhere, I mused, as I squinted toward some small specks along the beach.

"Do you vacation here, or live here all year round?"

"Both," he answered, not looking up.

How can that be? I wondered. *Maybe I'm asking too many questions. Or maybe he just doesn't want to tell me. But he seems friendly enough. I'll pursue it a bit further.* "What do you mean?"

"I'm retired."

"Oh, I see. So you live on the beach now, and life is a vacation to you."

"Right," he smiled at me.

He certainly had an interesting way of looking at things. I couldn't tell if it was a natural extension of maturity, or if it was his nature to be blunt and exacting. I was still wondering what profession he had been in. "What did you retire from?"

"Everything."

Here we go again! Oh, what the heck. I'll play his little game. But I must choose my words more precisely so he can't give me such an ambiguous answer.

"But not from fishing," I said.

"I hadn't fished until I retired." He got me there.

I tried again. "What profession did you retire from?" He couldn't get out of this one…but he did.

"Does it matter?" He asked, still staring at the pole.

I thought for a moment. *He must not want to tell me. He's done something shady and would rather not talk about it. It really is none of my business. I was prying, and his past has no bearing whatsoever on our conversation.*

"No, I guess it doesn't matter. Pardon me for asking." Then I was quiet for a while, thinking about what he had said. *Does it matter what occupation a person you meet at the beach has? It doesn't. The only reason you need to know a person's occupation is if you can use their services…but then…it does help to further a conversation if you have a mutual ground to work on. Maybe that is it. Maybe he doesn't want to discuss his occupation. Or maybe he just doesn't want to talk at all.*

I mused on whether he might have been a construction worker, or maybe retired from the oil fields. *He is tall and rugged looking. Why am I so compelled to find out what his occupation was? Is it necessary to categorize everyone by whether they are educated or not? Or whether they can help you in one-way or another? He is right. It doesn't matter.*

"English Teacher,"

"What?" I didn't know if he was stating what he was or conjecturing what I might be.

"I was a high school English teacher," he said matter-of-factly.

"Oh," I answered, a bit perplexed that I had envisioned him as a construction worker. Then, as they say your life passes in front of your eyes at the time of death, our conversation flashed back through, bringing with it the realization of what he was trying to do.

Whether by intent or from years of practice, he had made me think. No idle prattle. He had structured our conversation in a way to force me to plan out what I would say in order to get the desired response from him. This was good. As an analyst I needed this. I knew now that we would become friends. Though he had been difficult to talk to at first, he would be a challenge, which I needed at this point in my life. The challenge to think analytically, to not just analyze, but to anticipate and hypothesize before expressing. I did this with my patients, but not to the preciseness that this man demonstrated and led me to discover for myself.

I marveled at the teacher that he must have been. His students probably found him as cold and impenetrable as I had at first. I wondered how long it would take for a high school student to reach that same degree of enlightenment. It must have been a struggle for both them and him.

"If you don't mind me asking, it seems strange to me that an English teacher wouldn't be interested in the past…like that old house?"

"I have lived in the past for over fifty years." He was quiet for a moment. Then, as if just realizing that I was in my early thirties, he said, "That seems like a long time doesn't it?"

"Yes, it does."

"I started studying English literature in college when I was eighteen, and now I'm seventy. I retired a year ago. Now I'm through with it."

I thought of all of the books I wished I had time for. I have often said I'll do nothing but read when I retire.

"If you don't read, then what do you do?" I asked once more with ambiguity.

"Fish."

"Anything else?" I persisted.

"Eat and sleep."

"Is that all?"

"Walk on the beach…like you."

"Have you done any traveling?"

"That's traveling."

"No. I mean to Europe."

"To see a bunch of ancient ruins? I can look at myself in the mirror for that."

"You don't look like an ancient ruin to me."

"No. But I used to be. And now my life has changed. I've lived too long in the past. The Greek Myths, English and American novelists and poets: Elizabethan, Puritan and Victorian. I've read them all. They were exciting and enlightening, but now I no longer need nor read them. I've given up the past for the present. I now live, love and delight in the here and now."

"But surely, you must do *some* reading?"

"You sound like a teacher," he replied, scrutinizing me.

"No, I'm a psychoanalyst," I smiled.

"So…this is what fate has brought me!" He frowned at me, as if he were trying to decide on whether or not to take in a stray puppy.

"What do you mean?" I asked once more.

"Is that all you shrinks know how to ask is, *what do you mean?*" He mimicked me.

"No, of course not." He had me stopped again. I usually wasn't found at a loss for words, but this man had a way of depleting my thirty-four years worth of ego, and bringing it right back to puberty. I felt that I must defend myself by justifying everything I said. And I did.

"You act as if I'm trying to analyze you."

"Aren't you?"

"No, of course not. I'm just trying to be friendly. I hope you don't think I'm prying."

"Well, *you* seem to be asking all of the questions."

He was certainly right there. Then I realized that it was because he hadn't asked me about myself. Maybe he didn't care about me. Maybe he just wished that I'd move on and stop asking questions of him.

"I'm sorry. I'll stop bothering you." I started to back away.

"You're not bothering me." He looked up, smiling.

I felt like Alice with the Cheshire cat. Half expecting him to disappear before my eyes, I bluntly remarked, "If you don't mind me saying so, either you're crazy, or you really like to play games with people."

"Well, you ought to know. You're the analyst." He smiled widely, showing me deep-set dimples and a row of white teeth. A sparkle in his eyes made me realize that he was having fun. We both laughed and I leaned back over the weatherworn old piling and watched him fish.

We talked a bit longer, then we went our separate ways to our cottages on the beach. It was this summer I would discover that people come together for a purpose. There is a perfect plan in this universe, just as in the tides of the ocean and the rising of the sun. There is purpose in everything, though we may not recognize it at the time.

I walked up the short flight of steps to the sundeck of my rented beach cottage. On the deck sat a faded red lounge chair, two worn, aluminum beach chairs, a sun-bleached, weatherworn wooden table, and a rusty barbeque.

Now that the sun had completely disappeared, the ocean air had turned chilly and damp. I decided to go inside rather than sit on the deck in shorts as I often did in early evening.

A sliding glass door led into the small living room furnished in, what I called, Early Garage Sale and Late Goodwill – a stuffed couch slip-covered in orange; a green plastic recliner; a blonde coffee table and matching end table…antiqued with water rings and cigarette burns. The end table, which stood between couch and recliner, held a lamp of nondescript design – a brown piece of pottery with an under-sized yellow shade. The lamp and shade looked to have been picked up at a garage sale…separately.

A couple of kitchen chairs…one wooden and the other metal with a red plastic seat, sitting on the left-hand side of the living room, waiting patiently for company to come, so they might take their rightful places back at the kitchen table. There was no separation between living room and kitchen. Just a metal-legged, grey Formica table, which was pushed up against the stationary part of the sliding glass door, to allow for room to pass. And another red-plastic seated aluminum chair pushed under it.

The kitchen was modest. It contained the bare necessities for camping out at the beach. A door led out from the right side of the kitchen to a walkway, which followed along side of the house to the front where my car was parked.

I always had a problem distinguishing which was the front of the house and which was the back. Ordinarily, the front would be where you drive up to park your car. But there was no lawn or windows on that side of the house. So the back deck, which looked out to the ocean, was more like my front yard, because that's where people passed by, and all of the activity was.

To the left of the kitchen and the living room were a bedroom and small bathroom. This was ample room for me, as I was expecting no guests. I had brought my portable TV, my laptop computer, and lots of books to read. I had the bad habit of buying novels and not reading them. With so much to read on behavior and current theories in psychology, there was little opportunity to read fiction. But now on vacation, this was a wonderful time to catch up on some fun reading.

I changed into jeans and sweatshirt. Then, after making a tuna sandwich and pouring a glass of milk, I sat down at the table to eat and watch the waves roll in.

As the moon reflected off of the water, tiny iridescent fairy lights danced and sparkled on and between the whitecaps. Along the shore, the waves glowed with luminescent creatures as they were carried along in its bubbly denouement. I could see down the curved shoreline, beyond the dock to where the cliff descended. Tiny dots of light flickered along the coast, like fireflies queued up for the theatre - beach homes fading in the distance.

Wondering which small light represented the fisherman's house, I thought of what he had said about appreciating the present. That's what I was here for as well. For the last few months I had been throw into the past so totally and so emotionally, I knew I needed to get away to sustain my own sanity and sense of self-esteem.

Instantaneously, my thoughts flashed back to two years previously when my three-year-old little boy, Ricky, had been hit by a car, and later died in the hospital. Ricky had run into the street after a ball. The babysitter couldn't stop him in time. It was all too fast for anyone to prevent.

But, why? Why must we suffer such tragedies? Was it retribution for Tony's infidelity? Or was his infidelity the result of my lack of interest in him? Where does it all begin? And how does it finally end? Denial, defeat, depression, divorce. Then escape in order to forget. But, does one? Maybe...in time.

Wiping the tears from my eyes, I wondered what I would do this summer. In my two weeks here I had read, walked on the beach, played in the surf and sand, taken excursions into town, and spent many hours watching the tide roll in and out. *Will I get bored with all of this before the summer is over? Will I find enough things to occupy my mind for three months, so I can begin to live in the present again?*

I fell asleep that night, absorbed in an Agatha Christie mystery. There was no fear of imagining that someone might murder me in my sleep after reading Agatha Christie, because her mysteries weren't odious or ominous. They were more analytical in nature as a path was woven through old English countryside and manor house gardens. I think, I liked, more than the adventure, the environment. My heart would fly to Jolly Old England and search with Miss Marple or M. Hercule Poirot, through its pubs and curiosity shops, for the evidence that would lead me to the murderer.

Chapter 2

The Artist on the Beach

The next morning I awakened to seagulls screeching on the beach. The dream was still vivid in my memory:

I was in a used car lot talking to the salesman. He was distinguished looking, a man of authority. I had come for a car, a red Jaguar. It was an old car, but of great value. The age and design made it a classic, one that was appreciated very much by collectors.

I wanted the car, but wondered if I had the money for it. The salesman said, "It's yours." And he let me drive it off of the car lot without paying him any money. I wondered how he could have so much faith in me. But, I knew I would send him the money later. I remembered him saying it was only $300. It surprised me that I could have such an exclusive car for so little.

Then I remembered that my black Buick was at the car lot also. And for a fleeting moment, I thought I should have brought Tony along to drive it home. Then I realized that Tony and I were divorced and he wasn't anywhere around. I said to myself, "I don't need it anymore."

Driving off, I looked beside me and little Ricky was sitting with me, smiling very peacefully, as if to say, "Everything is going to be okay." The motor sounded loud and a bit rough at first, but then it smoothed out.

After thinking over my dream, so it was clearly in my consciousness, I wrote it down. Then I analyzed it so I would understand its significance.

As a psychoanalyst, I often use dream interpretation as a means of analysis and therapy. When we sleep, our thoughts continue sifting through our problems. Our dreams show us how we perceive ourselves and our problems, and if we understand the symbols, which are unique to our circumstance, we should be able to solve and resolve the inner frustrations that are plaguing us.

I have studied my dreams for a number of years. Often, when I first awaken, I might not see any sense to my dream, but as I begin writing it down, the truth comes to me.

This was the first time in a while that I had taken notice of my dreams. In San Diego my life had been so hectic with work, the divorce, Tony, lawyers, settlements, my parents and well-meaning friends trying to keep me busy, that I hadn't taken the time to sit quietly and listen to my inner guidance. In fact, that was the basic purpose of the escape to this Northern California coastline: to be where no one knew me, alone with my thoughts, able to sift out what happened, how it happened, why it happened, and what now?

Up to this point I had been asking myself just those questions. The two-day drive up the coast from San Diego to this little seaside town of Milton was spent questioning myself through various stages of denial, betrayal, anger, rejection, hatred, remorse, self-pity and grief. I wanted to be able to get on with my life. I had no intention of spending the summer wallowing in anger and resentment.

I knew all of the answers. I had used them many times in trying to help others. *He chases after other women because of his own lack of self-esteem. He knew you had a demanding career when he married you. Should you give up all that you value to make him feel better? It doesn't work, because the lack that he sees in you is really within him.*

I knew the answers, but couldn't accept them for myself. I still felt guilty that I wasn't able to make it work. As an analyst, I should have had the sensitivity to understand Tony. He was Sicilian – olive complexion, dark, mysterious eyes, and a winning smile. As an insurance salesman, he traveled extensively, visiting people in their homes. He was charismatic and people adored him. This gave him every opportunity to have an affair. But would a mature, self-assured individual be tempted? Possibly…if he thought his wife wouldn't be there when he got home, or if she were too tired to fulfill his needs.

But, is it necessary that a person's happiness be solely dependent upon what another gives to them? I knew that it shouldn't. I had told this to others so many times. Then why couldn't I accept this, and release the guilt, and get on with my life? For some reason, my inner being was not ready to accept. There had to be a greater insight, which reached deeply within me, before I could accept Tony's betrayal and deception as his problem and not mine.

I hated him! How could I not? He was screwing some woman when Ricky lay dying in the hospital. How could I forgive him?

Or was it my fault? Mine for not being there for him…for not desiring him enough.

How long did it take for one to forget and to go on without looking back? Maybe we never stop looking back. But, at last we reach a point in which we can look back without self-condemnation. The fisherman seemed to have left the past behind…starting anew. But, maybe he hadn't such anguish as I to forget.

Having written down my dream, I now looked for significance in colors, numbers, moods, feelings, personalities and symbols, as they were meaningful to me.

The first significant thing in the dream was the car lot. This means I am looking for a mode of transportation, something that will move me along in life. So, the purpose of this dream is to tell me how to get moving, rather than staying in my present standstill.

The car salesman is going to give me the answer. He is distinguished and a man of authority, someone I can trust and respect. This is my higher guidance.

I ask him about the red Jaguar. Why red? I began to free associate by thinking of what red meant to me. *A stoplight, a stop sign, a danger signal, a warning, a sign of anger, as in red-faced and hot under the collar. Yes, I guess that's me. This is telling me what is going on within me right now.*

Why the Jaguar? I don't know anyone with a red Jaguar…especially an old one. Then I remembered the Agatha Christie mystery. *That's why the red*

Jaguar. There was a much admired motor car in the story. That's why I dreamed about it!

I knew we often dream about seemingly insignificant things associated with movies, something we've read, or experiences we've had, because they are fresh in our minds and easy to identify with. These must not be passed off as insignificant just because they are the recollections of a movie or an incident. We must think of them as symbols, which we have chosen to symbolize an underlying meaning of something very significant to us.

In this dream, I wasn't really looking for the Jaguar. I seemed to know it was there, and I had come to get it. It was as if it had been all settled, and all I needed to do was pick it up. It was mine. I just needed to receive it.

That was my answer. This dream was telling me there was something of great value for me, and all I needed to do was recognize it and it was mine. Though it was almost priceless in value, for me, it cost very little. I could have it with no strings attached.

The Jaguar was very nice and very precious. But, why red? If red was anger or danger or warning, could that be precious? Our feelings are precious to us. Good or bad, we hold them in and nurture them until we don't want to give them up. Holding bad feelings inside is unhealthy. That's the danger…and especially when it is anger. That's the warning!

Why was Tony in this dream, when I'm trying to forget him? In the dream I said, 'I don't need it anymore,' meaning the black Buick. But actually, it refers to Tony. That's why I thought of him in relationship to the black Buick. The black Buick represents the black doubts, worries, fears, and mistrust I had with Tony. The dream is showing me I don't need that anymore. I'm through with those feelings, and must leave them behind, as you leave behind the old car, and drive out in the new one.

Numbers in our dreams are important messages. The number three refers to our wholeness…body, mind and spirit. Adding zeros to the number makes it stand out as very valuable. In this dream the $300 emphasizes the immense value of bringing body, mind and spirit into alignment. In San Diego and here I have been *wrapped up in my thoughts about the negative things that have happened to me. I have ignored my physical health and my spiritual well-being. But, here, at the beach, I'm bringing body, mind and spirit together.*

The red Jaguar represents something, which is very old and precious, something of great value. It is something you attain when you rid yourself of the worries and frustrations. That very special thing is peace of mind. What more could a person desire? It is very exclusive, very valuable, a treasure that costs nothing...but recognition. Is it that easy? Just to say, 'Forget the past' and it's over?

Then Ricky is in the car with me. He looks so much like his daddy...dark hair, small features and those big, round Italian eyes. He smiles at me, as if to say, 'Everything is okay.' Then I notice the motor sounds rough, but it soon smooths out. This means, although we have a lot of inner turmoil in the beginning, and things might seem rough, eventually it will all smooth out.

Ricky is a reminder to me that though his passing was very difficult for me at first, it has become easier now. It has been almost two years, and although it saddens me when I think of him, it's much easier to handle emotionally. In the dream, Ricky is saying to me, 'This too will pass.'

Yes! I must forget the past, and get on with the present. Like the fisherman, I must live in the here and now.

I dressed in shorts and shirt, ate an orange, and decided to go for a walk on the beach. As I walked out onto my deck, I felt the sun beginning to warm the atmosphere. Its rays slanted across surf and sand. I looked toward the dock to see if the fisherman was there. He wasn't. All was quiet. The only life on the beach were the grey and white gulls swooping down upon sea and sand groping for their breakfast, and little black, long-legged sandpipers running along the wet sand toward the water, snatching morsels left by the receding waves.

As I walked by, they scattered in a rhythmic dance of syncopated scurry and flight. Then I saw a figure, half-hidden in the shadow below the cliff. He stood at an easel with paintbrush poised in the air. He was looking right at me. At first I thought he was painting me, then I realized I was between him and his object...the dock.

"Oh, I'm sorry," I apologized, as I moved toward the cliff. "I didn't know you were there."

"Sometimes I'm not so sure I am either," he replied.

I thought, *Oh, no! Not another beachside philosopher!* But my curiosity overcame me. "Do you mind if I look?"

"No, be my guest," he answered congenially.

He was a handsome young man…tall and slim, with light brown hair. I walked around behind him to see his painting. He had roughly painted in the dock, the shoreline, and the cliff as it fades into the distance. I kept silent, not knowing whether or not my questions would bother him. I have a natural tendency to ask questions, having always been curious about things. My parents used to say that I would surely be either a lawyer or a college professor, so I could continue through life asking questions. However, an analyst does the same. It's necessary to know what's going on in order to help people.

The artist spoke first. "There's not much here. Just a beginning."

"But a great beginning! You've been painting for quite a while, haven't you?" I could tell this by how rapidly he mixed colors and filled in the spaces.

"Yes, high school, college and now I teach art at Milton High."

It was hard to believe that he was a teacher. He looked not much older than a high school student. He must have been about twenty-five or twenty-six.

"So, you spend the summer painting?"

"As much as I can. I also work part-time at *The Frame Up*."

"Oh, yes, the framing shop in town. Do you make frames there?"

"Yes. We frame pictures for people, and the owners allow me to sell my paintings through the shop."

"How on earth do you find time to paint?"

"Well, I like to try to catch the early morning sun and early evening sun for various effects. Then I teach eight to four. And I work at the shop weekends, except for summer. I put more hours in at the shop in the summer."

"Do you paint mostly out of doors?"

"Yeah, when the weather's nice. In the winter I do more portraits and still-life."

"Have you ever painted that old house up there?" I pointed toward the bluff. The house was out of sight. We were too close to the cliff to see it.

"No, I've painted other old buildings around here, but not that one. Thought I'd do it this summer. It's been up for sale for quite a while. No one lives in it, and the owners aren't around, so I can paint it without feeling like I'm trespassing."

"Do you know anything about the house?"

"Not much more than anyone knows. It was built by a sea captain in the Victorian days. He had two daughters who died there as old maids. It's been sold a few times throughout the years. You looking for a house?"

"No. I'm just on vacation, up from San Diego. I leased that little white house over there for the summer."

"You're alone?"

"Yes. No kids, recently divorced, and trying to get my head straightened out."

"That must be hell. I've never been married, but went through hell a couple of times breaking up."

"Yes, it is. But nothing ventured nothing gained." I surprised myself by saying that. Maybe that dream analysis did work. Maybe I was beginning to reconcile myself to the situation.

"That's for sure! You sure learn a lot from those experiences! But it's a hell of a way to learn!" He exclaimed, as he went on painting.

This young man is wise beyond his years, I thought. Then I watched silently as he detailed in various shades of the approaching sea: bringing the water to life with white caps and a huge wave, which rolled to the shore with translucent green reflecting through it, as it began to break and roll along the shore in white bubbly animation. He made it look so easy, as he swished the brush lightly across the canvas.

He had a keen eye. It was as if he were Svengali, beckoning with an intense glare and a flip of his wrist for the scene to leap onto the canvas in all of its vivid glory. He certainly had me under his spell. I watched in utter fascination as he wove his magic upon the canvas.

He wiped his brush and began to mix some colors on his palette. I wondered if my looking over his shoulder made him feel uneasy.

"Are you sure you don't mind me watching?"

"No. When I paint, I'm not aware of anything but my subject. When I teach, I often demonstrate to the kids. So I'm used to answering questions and having an audience. You should see me at the school carnival each year. I do charcoal caricatures, and you should see the swarm of people that crowd around me, especially kids. They come right up to my elbows. They're so curious. And they give a running commentary on everything I'm doing. It doesn't bother me a bit."

"That's amazing! I think you're a saint!"

"No. I just like kids. And I like my work. I figure if you don't like what you're doing, you should do something different until you find something you do like doing. So, what do you do in San Diego when you're not going through a divorce?"

I liked him. He had a sense of humor. He liked to ask questions. And he was philosophical. "I'm a psychoanalyst at the state hospital in San Diego."

"Uh, oh, I hope you don't do art analysis, or I'm in trouble."

"No. Don't worry," I laughed. "What little I've done certainly doesn't in any way relate to this beautiful painting. Besides, I don't try to psych out everything I see. It's funny, people always become defensive when they find out I'm an analyst, as if I could see right through them. But, I just concentrate on my patients, like you do with your painting."

Now the dock was coming to life, with clumps of seaweed and barnacles clinging to creosote-stained pilings. I marveled at how clearly he saw every detail from this distance. It challenged me to look more keenly, as he did. I tried to perceive which bit of detail he would include next. This was an adventure, a game, just as the conversation with the fisherman had been.

The fisherman had taught me to listen, and by thinking and anticipating, to better translate my ideas verbally. Now, by watching the artist, I was discovering how to perceive visually, and to mentally translate what I saw onto the canvas.

I began to wonder, if I watched long enough, if I would learn to paint. He made it look so simple. I felt as though I could do it. So, I asked him, "Is it possible for someone to learn how to paint by just watching you?"

"Yes, and with practice painting. I demonstrate certain techniques to my students, then they go to their easels and try it. Observation and experience, that's how we all learn everything."

"So true!" I vowed to take an art class some day. It wouldn't necessarily have to look exactly like something. I could just have fun dabbing paint on and make an impression of what I was seeing.

Later, as I walked on down the beach, I thought about this. *That's what we do in life…dab away…making impressions here and there, without establishing any real permanency. We go to work, associate, go home to our families, and relate to everyone in a way, which will keep peace. For what? If there is no growth, no expansion in our lives or relationships, then we are merely dabbing away at life.*

Chapter 3

The House Beckons

It was a beautiful day as I drove my black Buick into town. Sunlight glistened through the wispy trees, which skirted the highway into Milton. Every so often the trees would end, revealing a patch of green meadow with a farm or two, where horses and cows grazed a lazy noontime meal.

Wearing a flowered sundress and sandals, I quickly delivered letters to the tiny post office, and picked up a few items from the drugstore and deli. Then I headed back toward the beach. Reaching the turn off to my beach community, I saw it crossed the main road and continued along the cliff. Instead of turning right and winding down the hill to the beach, I headed the car to the left, where I was sure I would find the old Victorian house.

As the road lead further up the cliff, the houses became bigger and older. They were all very well kept - freshly painted, neatly trimmed lawns and hedges, and glorious arrays of flowers.

Then I saw it. The contrast was startling...a large, white, block structure, standing boldly among ruins of rose gardens, over-grown hibiscus and bird of paradise. The tall hedge surrounding it on three sides, looked as if it hadn't been trimmed in a year. I could barely see over it.

As I opened the black wrought-iron gate, it complained bitterly of neglect. A broken brick pathway led to the wide front porch. A large, double wooden door stood below a portico, held up by four wooden pillars. There were four tall, multi-paned windows – two to the left of the door, and two to the right. Four windows looked out from the second story, and four attic windows jutted out in gables from the roof.

I peeked through the windows on the left hand side of the door. I could see a long room with two fireplaces on the outside wall, tall windows beside them, and French doors at the far end of the room. This must have been a ballroom at one time. It was the full depth of the house.

I looked in the windows on the right hand side of the door, and that room looked like a living room or parlor. It had a fireplace bordered by tall windows, and was half the size of its counterpart. They were all hardwood floors. There was a double doorway into an adjoining room, which must have been the dining room. Crystal chandeliers hung from the ceilings of each of these rooms.

Then I stepped off the porch, and followed the brick pathway along the left side of the house. Because of the dense overgrowth of the hibiscus bushes, I couldn't see into the windows on either side of the fireplaces.

A wooden porch stretched across the back of the house, with screens rusted and wrenched from their frames. The porch had loose boards, which made me cautious with each step. I was intrigued by the French doors coming from the ballroom. They were locked, but I could see inside. At this end of the ballroom was a butler's pantry, which lead to the kitchen.

The large kitchen was between the ballroom and the dining room. Through the kitchen door and windows, straight ahead, I could see an old, wood-burning iron stove. A built-in bin next to it must have held wood or coal. On each side of the stove was a door, possibly to closets. On the right-hand wall were white cupboards, floor to ceiling, and a door and pass-through connected to the butler's pantry. On the opposite wall were white cupboards, which were the backside of the dining room china cupboards. A door there led into the dining room.

I envisioned the activity of the kitchen, bustling around the ancient stove, the cupboards, the preparation island, and the large, vintage, porcelain sink, near me by the window. Suddenly, a cold, damp breeze engulfed me. Startled, I jerked around, instantly aware that I was alone. Shuddering with cold chills, I stepped off the porch and into the sunlight.

Then I saw the gazebo. It glistened an antique white, as the sun's rays reflected from it. I walked the brick path through remnants of rose gardens and dried twigs hinting of a thriving vegetable garden long forgotten.

A tangled snarl of dried wisteria vines clung futilely to the gazebo's post and lattice. Unsure of its fragile support, I didn't venture inward. But, I appreciated its one-time splendor, and wished I might have enjoyed it in its glory.

Walking to the edge of the cliff, I could see where the stairway had gone down to the beach. Now a short chain-linked fence stretched across the bluff to keep pets and children from going over the edge. Below me, the fisherman was sitting on the dock, readying his line to plunk into the water. I yelled and waved, "Hey, down there!" He couldn't hear me over the roar of the ocean.

I turned and looked at the gazebo. Again, a sudden chill gripped me. All of the hairs on my body stood on end. Quickly, I hurried back to my car. But, before leaving, I copied down the name and number for Coast Realty's Sam Griffin.

From the deck of my beach house, I could see the fisherman was still there. Taking up the gauntlet of a renewed conversation with him, I changed into my beach uniform of shirt, shorts and bare feet.

Approaching the dock, I called out to him, "I was standing on that cliff yelling and waving to you a few minutes ago, but you couldn't hear me over the roar of the ocean."

"No wonder. I spend most of my time here in a meditative state. There's rapture on a lonely shore...and music in the ocean's roar," he smiled at me.

"I wondered why you came fishing here so much. I've never seen you with any big strings of fish," I teased him.

"You caught me, Little Lady. Now you know I'm a fake."

"I didn't say you're a fake. I just wondered if it wasn't a bit discouraging not catching anything."

"If I really wanted fish to eat, I'd go down to that seafood place on Main Street and buy some. Then I wouldn't have to gut and skin it."

"You are a fake all right!" I laughed.

"Not entirely. Just because I haven't caught any fish, doesn't mean that I won't. Remember, Young Lady, you haven't failed until you stop trying. Besides, I brought a rod and reel for you. I figured you'd be back to bother me. So, you might as well make good use of yourself."

"Well, you may have a hard time believing this, but I *can* catch fish. I go fishing with my father in San Diego. And I *have* caught fish! But that was on a boat in the ocean, not on a sawed-off slip of a dock like this, with waves crashing against it."

"That just poses a greater challenge, Little Lady." He grinned with wisdom beyond my understanding.

"Okay, but if I'm going to fish with you, we'd better be properly introduced. My name is Laura Christopher." I sat down beside him, picking up the rod and reel, and began putting an anchovy on the hook.

"Mine is Thomas K. Smith. But you can call me Tom. Say, I guess you *do* know how to fish! I was sure you'd want me to put the bait on for you."

"Just because I'm a girl?" I looked at him suspiciously.

"Christ no! I'm not *that* chauvinistic. But, let's face it. The questions you asked me about fishing the other day, weren't exactly profound."

"Well, I didn't know if the fish you were trying to catch from this dock were different from the fish out in the middle," I retaliated.

"How in the hell should I know? This is as new to me as it is to you."

"So, that's why you made those jokes about my legs."

"Right. I didn't want to show my ignorance."

"Well, you sure had me confused. I thought you didn't want to talk to me."

"You'll have to get used to my way of playing games. It comes from years of trying to get teenagers to think. And if you don't think *that's* a challenge, you ought to try it sometime!"

"I have. How about schizophrenic teenagers?"

"Aren't they all?" He scrutinized me with a hint of humor.

"Could be, Tom," I laughed. "Could be."

"What were you doing on the cliff…besides waving and yelling at this mottled mass of antiquity?"

"I stopped by that old house up there on my way back from town. I wanted to see it closer. It's for sale."

"You wanna buy it?"

"Well, no. I haven't even seen the inside. Besides…I don't have any money right now…not until the divorce is finalized. But I took down the name of the realtor. I *would* like to see the inside of it."

"What is it that fascinates you about that house?"

"I don't know. It's as if it's beckoning to me. It's almost as if it were a living entity. There's something about it. When I walked around the outside of it, I felt as though someone was watching me. It reminds me of a dream I once had about a house."

"And you still remember it?" Tom scrutinized me.

"Yes. I keep a journal of my dreams. I always write them down and analyze them. Usually houses are symbolic of the inner self. But this one was hard to interpret. I remembered it as possibly precognitive. I'm not sure. But, seeing that old house reminded me of it."

"So…you analyze your dreams? I thought dreams were just what analysts used for trying to figure out what's wrong with crazy people."

"Let's face it, Tom. We're all a little crazy in one way or another."

"Yeah, I can't deny that one."

"Sure. It's a fact that all people have problems of one sort or another. That's the reason we dream."

"To see how crazy we are? I always suspected it," he grinned.

"No, Tom, to help us figure out our problems. If you know how to decipher your dreams, they make a lot of sense. And they tell you a lot about yourself."

"Well, I'm glad I don't remember my dreams, or you'd be telling me I hate my father, and I had an Oedipal thing for my mother, with everything pointing to sex."

"Well, doesn't it?" I teased him.

He was quiet for a moment. Then, "Yeah, I guess it does all right. How did you know?"

"Because you said you didn't remember your dreams. But, I know you do, because the mind never sleeps, and body chemistry still goes on. The stomach stimulates hallucinogenic dreams whether we like it or not. And natural basic desires, especially in a single male, create dreams of sexual fantasies. And your denial was overt repression." I grinned at him knowingly.

"Jesus, Laura!" He blustered at me. "I knew I wasn't safe with you! Is nothing sacred with you shrinks?"

"Nothing," I laughed. "But, you don't have to tell me everything, you know."

"I might as well. You'll find out sooner or later, by some Freudian thing I say."

"I told you not to worry. I'm not going to psychoanalyze you."

"The hell you aren't! Every time you ask me a question, you're psyching me out!"

"That's funny, Tom. That's the way I felt about you...that you've been psyching *me* out." I grinned at him.

"You're right. I am. Isn't that what everyone does...put each other into categories? That's what you were trying to do with me the last time I was here fishing." He raised his thick, white eyebrows, and gave me a knowing look.

"You should have been a shrink, Tom."

"Oh, that rivulet of wisdom that trickles out of me at odd times, comes from spending one's lifetime trying to mold young minds, and reading the heart and soul of antiquated civilizations."

"You know, Tom, people come to me for help in putting their lives together. Now, with mine falling apart, I stand here in front of your ancient wisdom, feeling like a kindergartener."

"Ancient wisdom, huh? I hope you're referring to me as a conglomerate of knowledge, and not an outdated old fart."

"Yes, you're definitely a conglomerate," I laughed. "But, don't forget, you spoke to me first that night."

"Oh, I'd seen you moon more than once over that old house up there. Every time you come out of your beach house, you look up to see if it's still there. I figured it's like a phantom fascination for you, that you're not quite sure won't suddenly disappear."

"Somewhat. There is something about it that is beckoning. I want to know more about it. It has stories to tell. Don't you feel that?"

"The last thing I want to do right now is hear more old stories. I told you…that's what I've been doing the past fifty-two years…reading ancient literature."

"Tom, is that why you're sitting on this beach fishing," I asked quite seriously.

"There you go again, trying to psych me out." He looked at me, just as seriously. But, I persisted, for my sake as well as his.

"Well, usually, at least in my limited experience, when a person retires, he eases into his retirement gradually. He doesn't just give up everything he has been doing for fifty-some years and drop out of sight."

"So, now you can consider your experience expanded." He stared at his pole, as if to end the conversation.

"In other words, you don't want to talk about it." I looked questioningly at him.

"Hell, I might as well. You'll get it out of me one way or another." He looked at me with defiant resolution.

"Let's put it this way, Tom, we're both going to spend this summer right here on this beach…on this dock…fishing together. And I've already decided that we're going to be good friends, because I like you. Now, there is something special that we, as friends, can give to each other. And that is to share our thoughts and feelings, without restriction or predisposed judgment. What do you say?" I looked squarely at him, as he sat concentrating on his line.

After a few moments of silence, he said, "Okay, go ahead."

"Go ahead what?"

"Go ahead and tell me about yourself. Isn't that what you want to do?"

"Well, not exactly. But, it will do for starters."

I told him about Ricky's death and Tony's infidelity and my trying to lose myself in work at the hospital, then the final escape here, before my life disintegrated into chaos and psychosis.

Tom listened quietly, staring into the water, until I was finished talking. Then he looked at me with sensitive blue eyes. "You've been through a hell of a lot. I'm sorry. I thought you were just a curious kid who liked to ask questions about everything. But now I can see that you're actually searching for the meaning of life." He looked deeply and questioningly into my eyes.

"Well," I responded, "you certainly see a lot more than I do. You see a curious kid in a thirty-four year old body. And you see a search for the meaning of life in a few simple questions."

"That's true, Laura. I see it in you, because it's in me." He looked at me with serious intensity. Then he lightened up. "Now, that poses a good question. Do we only see in others, what we personally possess? You ought to know the answer to that one Doc."

"Just because I'm a doctor, it doesn't mean I have all of the answers."

"I'm glad you recognize that fact," he smirked.

"However, it is a psychological fact that we see in others what we like or dislike in ourselves. But, I'm not brave enough to affirm that we *only* see our own reflections in others. That's a pretty bold statement, and I'm not sure I have lived or studied long enough to know the answer. But, would you please explain how you see this quest for the meaning of life in both of us?"

"You lost a son. I lost a wife. Until we lose a loved one by death, life and death have little interest for us. But then, suddenly, through that loss, we wake up to the reality that there is another dimension to life. Then life after death becomes very important to us. That's what I meant by our common quest."

"I suppose you're right. I really hadn't thought of it in such a universal way. In fact, I always felt I was very alone with my feelings. I didn't share them much. I tried to share them with Tony, but he wouldn't talk about it at all. I knew it was important for us both to talk it out, but it's really different trying to help someone you live with, as opposed to someone sitting in your office.

"Now I can see it was much more than grief that he was holding in. There was so much guilt about him being with another woman when Ricky died, that he wasn't able to open up to me. And harboring those feelings led him to plunge into someone else's arms, searching for self-gratification…like an alcoholic."

"Like I did." Tom spoke softly, his eyes gazing at the water. I listened intently as he spoke of his wife. "My wife, Cecilia, and I had talked for years about traveling around Europe, and visiting all of the places we had lived vicariously…through books. It was the dream that we had been saving for. We were going to lease a villa the summer I retired… but…it never happened. She became terminally ill, and died the year before my retirement. So, I didn't retire. And I didn't travel. It didn't seem right, somehow…going alone. I asked myself *why* a million times. And could find no good reason to justify her death. She was a very special person…kind to everyone. So I plunged into new reading and reworking my lesson plans to keep my mind off of it. I took courses, to get my masters degree, so I could teach college at night.

"One day, last year, I looked in the mirror at an embittered old man, and marveled at how I could change so in just four years. How I was living did not solve my problem. I still couldn't reconcile my feelings. So I retired and bought a place here on the beach, in order to concentrate on me and my relationship to the universe. As Sam Coleridge said, *Work without hope draws nectar in a sieve, and hope without an object cannot live.*

"It begins with your immediate environment. Then you work out from there. You must first discover how you personally interact with the air you breathe, and those things you see, hear and feel, before you can take on the whole damn universe." He said this, not in anger, but as a challenge. He looked like Don Quixote, with tasseled hair and leathery face...set and determined. Then he went on.

"I think, now, I'm beginning to understand it better, this question of death. I mean...now that I've let myself settle down from all of the wild confusion of teaching. Here on the beach, I've been able to meditate about it. And opening up to myself, I have discovered a lot."

"Good! You can counsel me, then," I smiled hopefully.

"I guess that's about what I've been doing. Isn't it? I really didn't intend it that way, but once a teacher, always a teacher. Speaking of counseling, there's something you can help me with. When you were talking about dreams, I remembered a dream that Cecilia had. It's very strange and chilling. That's why it stayed with me."

"Sure, I'd be happy to help, Tom."

"It was when she was dying...not the last day, but she was in the hospital at the time, very sick. She told me she had a dream about *me* dying. I was in a coffin and she was looking down at me, and someone said to her something like, *It's okay, don't worry.* Can you imagine how I felt when she told me that? I must have gone ghostly white. I couldn't say a word, because I was so shook up about her dying, and that was the first time she had ever talked about it. Then she laughed and said, *Maybe that means you're going to die before I do.*" Tom was silent for a moment, possibly reliving the scene in his mind.

After a few seconds I asked him, "What did you say back to her?"

"Oh, hell, I said something really stupid, like *Damn it, Cecilia, stop talking so morbidly! You're going to pull through this and we're going to Europe this summer.* And she said, *I thought it was next summer.* And I told her we were going to go as soon as school was out. There was no use waiting another year.

"But she died before school was out. And I couldn't face summer without her. So I taught summer school, and went to night school to get my masters. That way my days and nights were filled, and I had no time to think about her and how guilty I felt about not taking her to Europe when we could enjoy it. We spend our lives waiting for the right time, without realizing that the right time is when the idea is first conceived."

"That's so true, Tom. If we could only realize it at the time."

"Wouldn't it be great, if we were given a copy of the script when we started out life?" he mused.

"It would sure make it easier!" I smiled faintly.

"Okay, now, tell me what that damn dream meant," he frowned.

"It's difficult to analyze a dream without knowing what was going on in the dreamer's mind at the time. I mean, how she thought and felt about her situation. But, I would guess that Cecilia knew she was dying. And she was worried about how you would do without her. Her dream showed you dead in a coffin, because subconsciously, she knew it would be very hard on you.

"The dream is telling her that you would go through a period of self-imposed death. You see, even though you were working like a maniac, you were dead to the reality of life. And, you were dead, or not aware of the reality of life after death."

"That's true. I was living in a state of unconsciousness. I knew she was in heaven. I believed in God. I had to, for her sake. But I hated Him for taking her. There was no sense to it. So I tried to ignore it. I couldn't deny God, but I could ignore him."

"I know, Tom. I did the same thing when Ricky died. Then we suddenly wake up and see ourselves. All things come right, eventually."

"If we just hang on long enough."

"That's what the last part of the dream is saying. It was telling her, *It's okay, don't worry. Tom will be dead to the reality of the situation for awhile, but then he will be okay.*"

"Yeah, I guess so. That makes sense."

"So, how are you doing now, Tom? Are you able to deal with it?"

"Christ Laura! You sound just like a shrink! Am I going to have to go through this all summer?"

"No. Not if you don't want to talk about it. Do you?"

"I might as well. You'll get it out of me eventually."

I smiled inwardly at his pretense of irritability with me, as he continued on.

"I moped around for awhile, trying to ignore God. But, as you can imagine, the beach is a hell of a place to come to if you want to forget God.

"You absorb the beauty and constancy of the tides, the sunrise and sunsets. You meditate on the sand and the creatures that make a life in it. And you hear the pounding of the surf day and night, and know there is a magnificent power that regulates things so perfectly, that life and death is no accident. There is purpose to life, and purpose to death.

"I wanted to know more about both, so I went to the library in town and checked out books on Eastern and Western religions, mysticism, psychic phenomenon, life after death, philosophy and whatever I could get my hands on."

"You *are* a fake! You told me you didn't read anymore."

"Well, I'm not, at the present. I read everything they have in that little library. And I just finished a paperback I bought in town. So really, I'm between books. I didn't want to get into it with you, because I knew you'd ask me what I'd been reading, and I'd have to tell you. Then you'd start arguing religion and metaphysics, and throw in doubts at a time when I'm still trying to absorb the concepts. Do you understand what I mean?"

"Yes, I do, Tom. I don't like to jump right into another book immediately after finishing one either."

"I suppose I should say I'm not reading about the past anymore. Now I'm reading about the present and the future."

"Oh, I see…sounds like a good idea," I mused.

Tom and I didn't catch any fish. But we had a good time discussing things. I guess that's the basic value of fishing anyway…meditating over one's experiences.

Later, when I returned to my beach house, I called Sam Griffin of Coast Realty. He said he would be happy to show me the Victorian house the next day. We decided to meet there at 10 A.M.

Chapter 4

Glimpses into a Faded Past

As I drove up to the old Victorian house, I saw that Sam Griffin's brown Pontiac was already parked in front, and he was standing beside it. He was a man in his fifties – salt-and-pepper hair, a friendly, round face with belly to match. He wore a Hawaiian short-sleeved shirt with grey dress slacks.

"Hi!" I called, as I climbed out of my car. "I'm Laura."

"Glad to meet you, Laura. I'm Sam."

"I hope you haven't been waiting long," I smiled, as we shook hands.

"Nope. Just got here."

Once again, the wrought iron gate shrieked in agony as it moved on rusted hinges. I followed Sam up the brick path and onto the porch. When he opened the door and stepped aside to let me enter, a whiff of dank mustiness filled my nostrils. I knew I must open some windows if I were to breathe in this house. Quickly, I turned to my left, entered the ballroom, and strode across the wooden floor toward the double French doors. I unlatched and flung them wide open, exclaiming, "Oh, I love French doors! Doesn't that ocean breeze feel wonderful?"

I spun around and walked back toward Sam. "Just imagine, men and women all dressed up in evening clothes, a small band playing over there, and drinks being served from the butler's pantry. How glamorous!"

"I don't know. I'm not so sure it was like that," he frowned uncertainly.

"Why?" I asked.

"Well, there were two old ladies that lived here. They were old maids. Their father built this place. The name was MacLean."

"But, surely, they must have had parties here at one time. Why else would they have a large ballroom like this?"

"Well, maybe in the beginning. But people I've talked to say the old gals kept to themselves...never went out."

"Were they invalids?"

"No. Neighbors saw them in the garden. But they never associated with anyone. They'd phone into town for groceries, and have everything delivered. Didn't even own a car. That's why there's no garage. There was a carriage house, but it fell down years ago."

"Were they the last people to occupy the house?"

"No. When they died, they willed the house to the convent, and the Catholics used it for a while. I guess it was too much to keep up for them, so they sold it. And a lot of furniture was donated to the museum in town."

"You mean, the ladies left their furniture to the convent too?"

"Yeah. Everything. They willed everything they owned to the convent. I guess they had no relatives to give it to."

"Wow! They must have been good Catholics!"

"No. I don't think they were Catholic. People say they never went to church. They just stayed here in this old house."

"Curious," I murmured, as I looked into a long narrow coat closet leading from the ballroom. It was dark, but I could see coat hooks lined up like little soldiers marching along the perimeter of the closet wall. A single light bulb dangled from the center of the high ceiling. I reached for an ancient switch, the kind you wind, but found the electricity was off.

"Here's the back way into the kitchen," Sam said, trying to move me along.

I could see that this door through the butler's pantry had been provided for servants to serve the guests in the ballroom. Maybe long ago, before they became spinsters, there were glamorous parties. I could imagine the tinkling of fine crystal glasses, the shuffling of crinolines and gay laughter.

Walking into the kitchen, I was amazed at how immense it was. The iron stove looked much bigger than it had from my peeking in the window. Built-in counters and cabinets had been freshly painted white. The upper cupboards all had leaded glass doors with antique white, round, porcelain knobs.

I opened the door on the right side of the old iron stove, thinking it to be a closet. There I found a narrow wooden stairway, which wound upward.

"Those are the servants' stairs to the second floor," Sam said. "See this row of lights here by the door? The servants could tell which room to go to by the light that was lit up. Eight lights, eight bedrooms."

"They must have had a big family."

"No, just the two girls. But, they probably wanted more. He was a sea captain. They say he built this house for his bride."

"How wonderful! I wish I could have lived here. When the parties were held, I mean." I peeked into the door to the left of the stove. It was a pantry.

"Yeah, I guess those were some affairs." He opened the door into the dining room. "Here, we can go through the dining room and living room, and go up the main stairs."

I followed Sam past the huge, dusty chandelier. The wide doorway into the living room parlor was framed in beveled, leaded glass. The sun's rays from the window, shone through the beveled glass, making a prism of color across the hardwood floor and onto the wainscoting of the far wall.

Opposite the front doors, a mahogany banister wound upward, leading us to the second floor. Again, I smelled the dank mustiness of closed up rooms.

"There were eight bedrooms up here originally, but then later they converted one room into a bathroom. I guess when it was first built, people still had outhouses and bedpans."

"Sam, I think they were called chamber pots. They were kept under the beds."

"Yeah. Chamber pots. I'm not sure if it was the Catholics that put in the bathroom, or the old ladies."

"Probably the sisters…the MacLean sisters, I mean. Not the nuns. I doubt whether they would want to traipse outside in the cold at their age."

"I don't know. They were pretty strange. No one around here ever saw them in town."

We walked from room to room. Four faced the front, and four faced the back. They all looked basically the same – high ceilings, tall multi-paned windows, faded wallpaper, and hardwood floors with wainscoting along the walls. A couple of rooms facing the front were newly painted and carpeted. Sam mentioned that the present owners had fixed these up.

I entered a room, which seemed sunnier than the rest because it faced toward the ocean. Two tall windows let sunshine pour across faded, threadbare carpeting. I followed the sun to the window, and stood looking out to the small sailboats bobbing on writhing waves. Below the veranda, I glimpsed the gazebo in bedraggled isolation, and the gardens, forlorn and desolate. I imagined the gardens in full glory, as my mind materialized rosebushes, honeysuckle, wisteria, tulips, bluebells, daffodils and daisies.

Suddenly a chill came over me, as if an icy hand had been laid on my back. Shaken from my reverie, I spun around, half expecting to see someone beside me. I found myself alone. Shuddering again, inwardly and outwardly, I quickly walked to the hallway where Sam was looking in some cupboards.

"These are for linens, I guess."

"Yes, that's nice." I followed him down the hall, keeping comfortably close to him.

"This is where the back stairs go down to the kitchen. Do you want to go down that way?"

I looked into the dark, dank chamber. "No. Thanks. I prefer the mahogany staircase. I'll pretend I'm Scarlett O'Hara when we go down." Then I saw another door. "What's this, another bedroom?"

"No. That's the attic. But it's locked and we don't have the key. I think the present owners had kids, and they locked it so the kids wouldn't go up there. They also put in that fence in the back."

As he was saying this, I had already taken hold of the doorknob and turned it. At that moment I felt as though I was surrounded by a chilling presence. Fear gripped me and I released the knob and moved quickly toward the stairs.

"Wow, it's cold up here," I exclaimed, beating Sam to the stairs. I scurried down and out into the sunshine, so fast that I didn't have time to reflect on how Scarlett felt as she descended the stairs at Tara.

I began to thaw out as we stood in the warm sun and discussed the house. "The owners are only asking $60,000," Sam said. "That's not much for a house this size, especially with a view of the ocean on one side and the mountains on the other."

I had to be honest with him. "Until my divorce is settled, I'm not able to purchase a house. But I love this one, and would love to have it. However, I must look for a mental facility where I can work. I doubt that Milton is big enough to support a private practice."

"Yep, that's what keeps people from buying here. Most of the sales are beach houses."

"I can understand that. I'm loving the little place I'm renting on the beach. It's so bright, sunny and warm. I have to admit, this house is a bit cold. I kept getting chills while we were going through it."

"Well, Laura, since you say you can't buy the house, I guess I can tell you this. The present owners have had a heck of a time trying to sell it. They've gone down in price three times. They'll probably go down again if it doesn't sell this summer, because it's almost impossible to sell a place like this in the winter."

I knew what he meant. If it was that cold in the summertime, how could he sell it in the winter?

"I guess people just aren't as interested in big, old houses as they are in beach places, huh?"

"Well, yeah, that's part of it. It has a lot of potential as a fixer-upper. But, I'll have to admit, people have told me that they got the same sort of feelings that you got in there."

"Didn't you feel different in there, Sam?"

"No. Can't say that I did. But, I don't believe in ghosts."

"Well, neither do I," I retaliated.

"I suppose people hear stories in town about the old ladies haunting the place, and it scares them away. The present owners painted a few rooms and carpeted them. But they wouldn't stay. I don't know…the place is in good shape, except for the backyard. The old girls got too old to take care of the outside, but there's no damage or neglect on the inside."

"Yes, the woodwork is in good shape…but…"

"But, it's creepy and cold. Right?" He grinned at me.

"Right!" I agreed, shuddering at the thought of that cold hand on my back.

"Well, I wouldn't cheat anybody. I want my clients to know I'm on the up and up."

"Thanks, Sam. I trust you. And if I had the money and a job here, I would seriously consider buying it. But I have to be where I can make a living."

"Yeah. I understand. You keep my card, though. Tell your friends to look me up."

"I sure will, Sam. Thank you."

Sam went back in and closed the French doors I had opened. As I maneuvered my car around to leave, I couldn't drive past the house without stopping to look once more. There was something foreboding about it. Yet, there was a lonely beckoning to it, as well. I knew I would come back, if only to look at the outside, and dream of a bygone era.

When I reached the end of the road, where the Milton highway divided the cliff houses from the beach houses, I didn't want to go home. Instead, I drove into Milton and looked for that museum where the MacLean sisters' furniture was stored.

The museum was just a part of an old warehouse that had one side converted into a museum, and the other side stored old farm machinery. It was small, but there were two floors, and plenty for me to look at.

Behind a wooden desk, sat a lady in her late fifties, who managed the museum. Her hair was tightly permed and naturally grey. She was slightly taller than my 5'5", and neatly dressed in a maroon pantsuit and heels. This lady was a well of information. While waiting for people to drop in on her, she studied history books and genealogies. I must have been the first person she'd seen that day, for she jumped up from behind her desk, handing me a brochure, and introduced herself.

"Welcome! I'm Vivian Hendricks, manager of the museum. Here is a brochure that tells how the museum is laid out. Each room is organized into a certain era: Early Indians and Spanish settlements down here, with Civil War and Victorian upstairs."

"I am interested in the Victorian era," I said, as I headed toward the stairs.

Vivian followed me, acting as my tour guide. "Milton was originally called Mill Town, because it had a lumber mill here. But, that closed a long time ago. Then people just shortened it to Milton."

"Do you know anything about Captain MacLean and his spinster daughters?" I asked.

"Oh, yes, of course. Captain Andrew John MacLean came from Scotland in 1881 with his new bride, Katherine. They arrived in San Francisco, where he was captain of a cargo vessel to England. He had a mansion built here for Katherine out on the cliff. Many sea captains built their homes on the cliff. They liked to look out to the sea. His was one of the first ones around here. Their first child, Annabelle, was born on June 5, 1883. One year later Elizabeth was born on May 18, 1884. Here is the room where their furniture is displayed."

She led me into a room full of nineteenth century furniture. The furniture was arranged into a bedroom, parlor, study and dining room. A huge armoire, a four-poster bed, two nightstands, a dresser, a commode, a writing desk all matched with three-toned inlaid wood. Lace doilies and knickknacks sat upon the dresser and nightstands, while a large, flowered pitcher and basin graced the marble-topped commode.

Vivian still stood beside me as she expostulated over the grand houses that the sea captains had built on the cliff. "…each trying to out-do the other. They built here because Captain MacLean did. He had a dream of Mill Town becoming another San Francisco. The mill attracted the captains with their ships. That's why he built that big dock. But when the mill died out, things shifted back to San Francisco.

"They brought all of their furniture, from all over the world, by way of that dock. They hauled the big stuff up the cliff by pulleys. It was hard, but faster than waiting for wagons to come and haul it through muddy roads.

"Then in 1889 Katherine died of pneumonia, leaving the captain with two small daughters. It must have been very sad for the two little girls, especially with their father out to sea for months on end. Of course, they had servants to take care of them – housekeeper, cook, gardener, livery boy and governess."

"Did they ever have any big parties at their house?"

"Well, of course when they were older they didn't socialize at all. In fact, the only person allowed at the house was the delivery boy who brought them groceries. I'm not even sure if he went inside. He may have just left the groceries on that big back porch by the kitchen door."

"Oh, you've been out there then? You've seen the house?"

"Yes, inside and out. I try to get to all of the places I tell about. That way I can make my stories more real."

"I went inside it today," I offered.

"Are you thinking of buying it?"

"No. I can't afford it right now."

"Me neither. Besides, I'm all alone, and what would I do with a big, old, cold house like that? I couldn't afford the heating bill alone." She waved her hand in futility.

"But, it does fascinate me," I added. "It makes me want to find out more about it. Do you think they ever had grand balls there?"

"Possibly, when the girls were growing up, and in their teens. That's what people did in those days to help their daughters find a husband. They would throw a big coming-out party when they turned sixteen. And they'd invite all of the eligible young men in town."

"But, they didn't marry. I wonder why. They must have had plenty of money to socialize and travel, by the looks of this furniture." We were standing in front of an enormous dining room table. It was set with china, silver, large silver serving platters and candelabra.

"Yes, they lived their whole life off of what the captain left them. And there was still plenty of money given to the Catholic Church. The convent has a lot of things too. They kept the smaller pieces of furniture, and the nicer sets of silver and china. This stuff is what they used for everyday. You can tell. It's fairly worn. But it's perfect for here, because people come here to see old stuff."

"Do you have any pictures of the sisters?"

"No. We don't. But the convent has an album and some personal things that they are keeping. I don't know what for. They'd do more good here where people could see them. You should go out there. The nuns are very friendly. They showed me all around the place, and I'm not Catholic. You know where the Holy Sisters of Saint James Convent is, outside of town, north of Milton?"

"Yes, I've seen their sign."

"Why don't you stop there and ask about the album. They'll let you see it. They showed me lots of things they've been given from different families around here. They are very nice."

"Thanks, Vivian. I'd like that. By the way, were the MacLean's Catholic?"

"It's funny, but I never asked. I just assumed they were. They must have been. Why else would they leave everything they owned to the church?"

"Well, I was told they didn't go to church. But that could be wrong."

"Very often older people can't get themselves to church. Especially living clear out there by the beach. Say, why don't you check with the Catholic Church? They keep records of the families in their parish. And if you want to find out about the parties, check with the Milton Register. That's the original newspaper, and they have the old papers on microfilm."

"That sounds like fun, Vivian. Maybe I will look at some of those old newspapers. I have nothing better to do with my time."

"How long will you be here?"

"I've leased a place on the beach for the summer. There isn't much to do out there but walk, read, fish and lie in the sun. I have to be careful of that, with my fair skin. I think it might be fun to find out the history of that old house. There is a certain mystery about it that is begging to be solved."

"That's great! Be sure to let me know what you find out. Every little bit helps with my guided tours. And if I can help you in any way, please phone me. My number is on that brochure."

"I sure will, Vivian. Thank you for your help."

"That's what I'm here for," she smiled and walked me to the door.

Leaving the museum, I headed straight for the newspaper office. In contrast to the old wooden warehouse where the museum sat, the Milton Register building was a one-story, modern concrete structure, with big windows across the front.

When I asked the pretty, young brunette at the front counter if I could look at some copies of old newspapers from the late 1800's, she left and brought back a man whom she introduced as Bryan Lewis. He was in his mid-thirties, light brown hair, brown eyes, of medium build and wearing jeans and tee shirt.

When I explained what I wanted to do, his face brightened in a congenial smile. Then he led me to a file cabinet in the back of the room.

"Here, these are the newspapers from 1880 to 1910." He pulled out a drawer full of microfilm. It was hard to conceive that 20 years worth of newspapers could be put into a small drawer. He set the drawer down on the table next to a machine.

"Do you know how to work the microfilm reader?"

"Yes. I'm a psychologist. We use them a lot at the hospital for reading case histories."

"Are you doing some research for one of your cases?" He leaned against the table and looked questioningly at me.

"No, I'm vacationing here…getting over a divorce. I live at the beach, and am fascinated with that old MacLean house on the cliff. Do you know it? It's the one for sale."

"Oh, yeah, the big white one. You interested in it?"

"Well, not to buy. But there is something about it that fascinates me. It's as if it were beckoning to me to come and find out more about it."

"I know what you mean." His eyes brightened as he spoke in a low voice. "Buildings do that to me too. Maybe that's why I became a reporter. Places and things intrigue me, urging me to investigate them. How are you going to go about this?"

"Well, I visited the house with Sam Griffin from Coast Realty, and that huge ballroom captured my attention. They wouldn't have built it if they hadn't planned on having parties there. And people in those days had coming-out parties to enable their daughters to meet young men. Now, I'm wondering why the sisters never married. And why they never left that house. Doesn't that seem strange that they never left the house or let anyone in?"

"Maybe they were ugly," he smiled.

"No one is *that* ugly! Besides, they gave everything they owned to the convent, and they weren't even Catholic."

"Are you sure of that?"

"Of what?"

"Of everything you said – that they didn't have parties, never married, never left the house or let anyone in, and gave everything to the convent and weren't Catholic?"

"Well, no. I'm not sure of it all. It's just what people have told me. But, Vivian Hendricks at the museum seems to know a lot about this town…"

"But, it's all rumor until you personally verify it."

"I know. That's why I'm here."

"You should check the church records and the convent records. They have a private chapel at the convent that the MacLean's might have gone to. But don't take anyone's word about it. You've got to check everything."

"I have all summer. I just might do that," I smiled at him, not entirely sure of myself.

"And I'll help you when you get stuck. Okay?"

"Yes, thanks, but I don't want to keep you from your work."

"Don't worry. We don't have a lot going on around here. They can spare me. Now, where are you going to start?"

"I thought that since Annabelle was born June 5, 1883, she would have her coming-out party at age 16 of the same month. So, if I look at the newspapers the first week of June 1899, I should find an article about her party."

"Right. Also check the following week, in case there's a follow-up story."

"I will. And then I'll check May 1900 for Elizabeth's."

"Okay. I'll come back later and see how you're doing. If you need anything else, just ask Karen at the front desk."

"Thanks, Bryan. I appreciate all of your help."

"Your servant, Ma'am." He made a sweeping gesture like D'Artagnan, and backed away.

Settling into the microfilm search, I found a follow-up story of Annabelle's coming-out party. It sounded as if every young man and woman in town attended. There were even some from San Francisco. It was quite an elegant affair.

Then I looked for Elizabeth's party. There was nothing written in the May 1900 papers at all. Thinking I may have made a mistake on the date of birth, I checked all of 1900 and 1901 papers. There were four coming-out parties held in 1900. Each article said Miss Annabelle MacLean and Miss Elizabeth MacLean were unable to attend due to illness. These parties were held months apart. I wondered if one of the girls or their father had suffered from a long illness.

I put the file drawer back. As I was about to leave, Bryan Lewis came out of his office and asked me how I had done on my search. I told him what I discovered, and he recommended I check the clinic to see if they had any records of a prolonged illness at the MacLean house. I wasn't sure if I wanted to delve into it that deeply. I hated to bother people for this silliness. After all, I wasn't going to buy the house. Bryan and I exchanged business cards, and promised to keep in touch.

Later that afternoon, I called Vivian at the museum to let her know what I had discovered at the newspaper.

"Oh, I'm glad you called, Laura. You made me curious about the picture album. I thought it would be nice if I could get some pictures for our display, so I called the convent. One of the nuns there said they had an album of the MacLean's, but it was willed specifically to Sister Mary Angelica, and was to be kept at the convent. But, she said you could look at it if you want to."

"Thanks, Vivian. I think I will. Something I wanted to ask you was, if you knew of any prolonged illness in the family, possibly when they were in their teens?"

"No, I haven't heard of any. But, I'm sure that is the only thing that would keep a young lady from a coming-out ball in those days. There just weren't that many opportunities to socialize in this area."

"Well, I'll check at the convent, and see what they can tell me."

"Good. And please keep me informed, Laura. The history of this area is my life's work. Anything you find out, pass it on to me. Okay?"

"Yes, I sure will, Vivian. Talk to you later. Bye."

That evening Bryan called to see if I had checked with the clinic. I hadn't. I told him I felt silly snooping around without any concrete reason.

He said, "Curiosity *is* a concrete reason. Any time you want to find out something new, you set up a certain pattern of energy, which makes things fall into place for you. It's like a scientist searching for a reason for something. We all have that innate curiosity in us. And it's gratifying to find solutions. That's why I want to help you find your answers."

"It's hard to find the answers, when you don't even know what the questions are, Bryan."

"Well, you told me that old place seemed eerie and beckoning to you. You wondered why the sisters never married and never came out in public. Those are good questions to start an investigation with. We could look at more old newspapers to see if anything went on at that place, but it would take a long time searching that out. Your best bet is to find out what the nuns know."

"Yes. I plan on doing that sometime this week."

"Then another good source is the county census, because it tells births, deaths & marriages...besides listing all of the people who lived in the house, and what kind of work they did."

"That sounds like fun. Where do I find it?"

"At the county courthouse in Northport. Want me to take you?"

"No thanks, Bryan. I'm not sure when I'll go. But I'll let you know what I find out."

"Good! We'll make an evening of it...dinner at the Charthouse. I'll interview you as a student of historical houses...delving into the past of the MacLean house. That ought to interest the subscribers. You never know, someone might come forth with some information."

"Oh, I don't know, Bryan. I don't want to make a big deal out of this. If I find the time, I'll explore. If not, I won't. It's just that simple."

"Well, we could still go out to the Charthouse. Have you been there?"

“No.” I didn’t know what to say. I didn’t want to go out with him. He wasn’t bad looking, in an ordinary sort of way. But, I hadn’t dated in seven years, and I didn’t feel as though I was ready to, quite yet.”

“Then maybe Saturday, if you’re free. Okay?” He sounded hopeful. I hated to disappoint him.

“I don’t know, Bryan. I’ll see.” I didn’t want to encourage him. I really wasn’t ready to start dating. Guess I was still a little gun-shy. I had heard plenty about guys who prey on divorcees, because of their vulnerability. I didn’t want to be vulnerable to anyone, just then, anyway.

Chapter 5

Meeting the Mystical

I spent the next few days reading and walking on the beach. At one point, as I looked up at the old house on the cliff, I realized I was getting just like the sisters. I did not want to leave my house to go check on the church records, the census records, the clinic or the convent. Maybe they didn't leave their yard because they had everything they needed right there – a beautiful house, lovely gardens, and a view of the changing colors and patterns in sun, sky, sand and surf.

Once more, the enchantment of a bygone era drew me to it. I needed to stand on the cliff, and envelope myself in forgotten fantasies of the past. So I did. I drove my car to the house on the hill, and was surprised to see a van was parked there. The gate was open, so I entered and walked around to the back of the house.

Then I saw him…the artist. He stood near the gazebo, with easel, palette and brush looking up at the house.

"Hi, David! So you finally made it up here."

"Hi, Laura. Yeah, I've been working up here for a few days. What do you think?" He stood back to give me a full view of his work. It was the backside of the house, bright, happy and surrounded by flowers. There were lacy curtains in the bedroom windows, and from behind one curtain, there was a figure of a woman.

"I love it! But you put a woman in the bedroom window."

"Yeah, I see her there. She's looking at me with a mystical expression on her face. Do you see her up there?" He looked up at the window.

"No. I wish I could." I strained my eyes at the window. "Are you psychic?"

"No. I just like to put a little extra into my paintings…to kind of surprise people with the unexpected."

"Well, you surprised me all right. She looks as if she belongs there."

"That's the idea. I let my imagination take over, and sometimes, even I'm surprised at what I come up with."

"David, I'll bet you *are* psychic."

"Why do you say that?"

"Because that is the very window I stood in the other day, and…now don't think I'm crazy…but, I felt a hand on my back. I was left with the impression that I was intruding into someone's private place."

"You probably were." He continued painting without looking up.

"Huh?"

"Well, I've read a lot of books on ESP. A sudden, cold chill that someone has touched you with an icy hand, is supposed to be just that. Sometimes the spirit world wants to get in touch with us. It doesn't happen very often to most of us, but if the vibes are right at the time, communication can happen, either by touch or hearing."

"Don't tell me you've heard voices, David!"

"No, not me. But I know a lady that really is psychic. She's a very plain sort of lady. You'd never know by just looking at her."

"What can she do?"

"She can tell fortunes, and find things that are lost."

"How does she do it? Does she read tea leaves or look into a crystal ball?"

"No. Nothing like that. She doesn't wear funny clothes or make a big deal out of it. She's the mother of one of my students. I had lost my class ring, and it didn't show up for a week, so I asked in all of my classes if anyone had found it. After school, this one boy, Kyle, said his mom could find it for me. He said she was good at finding things. I told him it was good to have a talent like that. Then I forgot about it. Later, one day, he showed up with his mom. She held my hand, touching where I wore my ring. Then she walked over to the box where the pile of rags was kept. She reached down into the rags, feeling around, then pulled out my ring. I had laid it on the shelf above there when I was turping my hands. And it got knocked off into the box."

"That's fascinating! I've never met anyone who is psychic…at least, that I was aware of, anyway. I firmly believe in the extrasensory sensitivity of some people. Although, I've never been able to see it in myself."

"Being an analyst, you're probably more analytical. To be sensitive to the vibes of the universe, you've got to go with the flow. Get into your right brain, and let your intuition take over."

"Like you do in your painting?"

"Yeah. That's what I do, without even thinking about it. I think that's the clue. You just have to not think, and it puts you into a meditative state, which opens you to your extra senses."

"I guess you're right. You know, I felt very close to communication when I was in that house. I suppose it was because I was letting my mind imagine how it had been living there with the gardens in full bloom. That's when the hand touched me."

"Yup, that was a psychic experience all right. Have you found out anything more about the house?"

"Yes. A sea captain, Andrew John MacLean from Scotland, built it for his new bride, Katherine. They had two daughters, Annabelle and Elizabeth, who became spinsters and never left the house. Isn't that weird?"

"Yeah. I wonder why they didn't go out."

"I wonder why, too. Their mother died of pneumonia when they were young. I found in old newspapers, that Annabelle had a coming-out party when she was sixteen, but Elizabeth didn't. It was the year following her sixteenth birthday that Annabelle stopped going to parties. I wish I knew why."

"If you really want to find out, maybe Mrs. Erickson can help you."

"Who is she?"

"The psychic mother that found my ring. We could take her into the house and see what she senses about it."

"Really, David? Do you think she would?"

"Sure. I think so. She's a nice lady. Very humble about her gift."

"Okay then, I'll call Sam Griffin and see when he can take us through. Then I'll call you, and you can call Mrs. Erickson."

"Fine. My number is 596-4033."

I wrote his number down, then looked once more at his painting, then up to the corner bedroom window. I wished I could see the lady in the window. I squinted and stared, but nothing. So, I said goodbye to David, and left.

Sam Griffin was agreeable to letting Mrs. Erickson *psych out* the house. We agreed that maybe this is what the house needed…a good old fashioned exorcism. I called David and he said Mrs. Erickson was happy to help us.

In the meantime, Bryan, from the newspaper office, called to see what I was doing Saturday. Joking, I said, "I'm going to a séance."

He said, "Great! Can I come too?"

It surprised me, but I said, "Yes. It's at the old MacLean house on the cliff…at two o'clock."

So, Sam, David, Mrs. Erickson, Bryan and I met outside the Victorian house Saturday afternoon. David had brought Mrs. Erickson, and he introduced her to everyone. She was quiet and shy, but with a warmly sincere smile. I liked her immediately. She was in her late fifties or early sixties, plump, with a serene round face and greyish-brown hair. She wore a long, flowered, short-sleeved dress and sandals. She looked like someone's mother. I never would have guessed her to be psychic. But then I didn't know what a psychic was supposed to look like, anyway.

As David introduced us, I put my hand out to shake hers. She held my hand in both of hers and said, "This too, will pass." I knew what she meant, as Ricky and Tony flashed before my face.

I smiled and said, "I know. Thank you."

As we entered the house, that same musty smell wafted into my nostrils. This time I didn't run for the French doors, because I didn't want to disturb the vibrations that Mrs. Erickson was trying to sense.

She walked the same route that Sam and I had walked…into the ballroom, where she stopped, facing the fireplaces. "The joy went out of this room long, long ago…too long ago," she said solemnly. Then she led us into the kitchen, and opened the stairway door, looking up the servant's narrow staircase. "There is a feeling of secrecy here… much secrecy."

We went through the dining room and parlor. She stopped and turned slowly around in each room, but said nothing. We followed her silently, waiting, listening, in enchanted expectancy.

She walked slowly up the stairs, sliding her hand along the banister, as she went. "Not many happy times. Sadness…regret…loneliness."

At the top of the stairs she went to the left into the room that was neatly carpeted and painted. "Little children played here. Not long ago. Then they left."

We went to the next room. It was carpeted too, and newly wallpapered. "The parents of the little ones slept here. 'It's too cold here,' she says. 'Okay,' he says. 'I can do better closer to the city.' And they left."

Then we followed her to the next room, which was in its original state. The antique carpeting was worn thin, but the velveteen, rose-patterned wallpaper still remained in good condition. Mrs. Erickson ran her hands along the walls, as if they could communicate with her in braille.

"This lady was proud. She was loyal and faithful. She ran the house. Everyone did what she told them to do." She took a last look around before leaving this room. "Yes. She was the boss."

In the next room, the one in which I felt cold, Mrs. Erickson said nothing at first. She stood in one spot and looked from place to place in the room, as if picturing where the furniture had been, or maybe following a phantom figure, as it glided back and forth across the room. She said nothing. She seemed to be listening.

Then she briskly walked to the window, and looked out. "Yes, there it is...the gazebo. Such sadness here...rejection, loneliness, a broken heart. Hours of watching at this window...and out there in the shelter of the gazebo. Not the same woman...a younger woman...a lost life. So much to live for, but barely living. Just existing."

Then she turned from the window. "But, that was another era. Things were different then."

I wanted to ask her to explain, but I was afraid I would disturb her concentration, or maybe my voice would jumble up the vibratory patterns of the house. I didn't know what was going on here. So, I kept quiet, just to be on the safe side. I think we all felt that way.

As the others filed out of this room, I was caught up in thought about what life was like within these walls. Somehow, I was the last to leave the room. As I neared the door, a cold dampness surrounded me. The hair on the back of my neck stood on end. I felt like a cat on tiptoes, hunched-back and stiff. For a moment, I was unable to move. Shuddering, I quickly ran out of the room and hurried down the hall to catch up with the others. I hoped it wasn't following me.

Mrs. Erickson had her hand on the doorknob to the attic. "We must find the key. It's important that we look up here."

"I'll have to get it from the owner. They live in Northport. I can run over and get it this week." Those were the first words from Sam, other than a few whispers to Bryan. I was surprised that he was so agreeable. But, when we were once again outside, he said, "This is good. If we can get the mystery of the MacLean sisters cleared up, I'll be able to sell this house."

David said, "I've read, that when the problem is out in the open about a place, then the spirits are satisfied, and they move on."

"Yes," said Mrs. Erickson. "And remodeling sometimes moves the spirits out. That's why I felt the present owner's vibrations in the modernized bedrooms."

"Can you tell us why the sisters made recluses of themselves?" I asked her.

"I don't know the whole story. I sense that the young one was rejected. She waited and waited for almost her whole life for someone to come back. But, he didn't. She watched to the sea for him."

"Could that be her father?" Sam asked. "He was a sea captain."

"No, not her father. There is more passion in it than between a father and a daughter. It was someone she loved and pined for. There is remorse and regret in that room. And there is a link to the gazebo."

"Come on," I said. "I'll take you to that." I wanted to see what vibes she got from the gazebo.

Mrs. Erickson carefully walked into the gazebo. Picking up a twig, she brushed old spider webs aside, and sat down on a built-in bench. "Yes. It was here that she sat and waited. She could see the ships come into the dock from here. The dock was much longer then. Ships would unload goods down there. There were steps going down to the beach. She thought he would come back."

"Who was he?" Bryan asked.

"They were lovers. That staircase from the kitchen to the bedrooms, she would come down that way at night, and secretly meet him here in the gazebo. Sometimes they would sneak down the steps to the beach."

We were all quiet for a moment, as we looked toward where the steps went down to the beach. Then Sam said, "Well, if there's no more, it's getting late. I'd better get home to dinner."

"Yes," we all agreed.

As I was getting into my car, Bryan asked, "How about you and me getting something to eat in town?"

"Oh, thanks, Bryan, but I've got stuff in my fridge that I have to eat, before it takes on a life of its own."

"Do you want help eating it?"

"I'm sorry, Bryan. Not tonight. But thanks."

"Okay, but I'm going to keep trying."

"Okay," I smiled, and drove off.

As I sat alone on my deck, sipping a cup of tea, and watching the shimmering waves roll along the shore, I thought of what Mrs. Erickson had said. *Elizabeth pined for her lover, who went to sea and never came back. Maybe that's why she didn't have a coming-out party. She was waiting to marry her lover. And Annabelle stood by her. Mrs. Erickson said the older one was loyal. She said she ran the house, too. Maybe Elizabeth became sick from remorse. Maybe she was weak and needed the constant care of her older sister. Would Annabelle give up everything for her sister? Elizabeth might give up everything for an unrequited love. But, would an older sister lock herself up from the world for her younger sibling? I must find out. I'll visit the convent tomorrow.*

That night I had a dream. *I was driving my car down a dark road. Then I went up a hill and saw a big, old Victorian house. It didn't look like the MacLean's house. It was white outside, with paint peeling off of it. There was a dilapidated picket fence around it. The gardens were old, and unkempt. I opened the gate and walked in. A pathway led me through remnants of snarled weeds and dried twigs. As I made my way through the maze of dead plants, I thought, "This was once a beautiful garden. All it needs is some water and care."*

Then the path led me to the house. I walked up the rickety steps. I was unsure of my footing. The steps looked like they could fall in. The house was very plain on the outside. It looked like it hadn't been lived in for many years.

As I opened the door, I was surprised to see the interior was all aglow with lights and color. It was a similar design as the MacLean house, but bright with color and light. A shiny hardwood floor greeted me, with a huge golden chandelier hanging from the ceiling. Behind it I could see the stairway going up.

To the left was a ballroom, and a party was going on. I saw a young lady in a beautiful, flowing white gown. I thought I had been transported into the nineteenth century. Then a lady, whom I didn't know, came up to me and said, "This is right." I said, "Yes," knowing she meant this is the way it should be. But then, I noticed that she had on modern-day clothes. I thought that was very curious. Then I awakened.

I lay there and thought about my dream, to get it firmly planted in my consciousness. Then I wrote it down, and started to analyze it. I knew that the interpretation of a dream could be either subjective or objective. In subjective interpreting, you must take all people, situations, feelings and statements, and relate them to the dreamer's inner struggle with self. In objective interpreting, the analyst relates the people and situations to the dreamer's actual relationships with others.

Because this dream began with me driving my car, I knew it was referring to how I was handling my life. I'm in the driver's seat, behind the wheel. I'm in control of my life. No one is controlling me.

But, there is more of a lesson here. I'm in control of my life, but I'm in the dark about something. That means I'm unaware or closed up to an idea or situation.

Going up hill is elevating my thoughts. It's bringing things into consciousness by thinking in a loftier mode.

A house can be part of a certain experience, situation or relationship. Or, it is a representation of the dreamer. The house is where we live. What is going on outside of the house is what is happening outside of me, or how I'm relating to my outer world. What is shown on the inside of the house is what I'm personally developing, in attitudes and feelings about myself. We see ourselves and our ideal selves in our dreams.

So, this dream is saying that, though I am in the driver's seat and in control of my life, I am still in the dark about some things. However, driving uphill is elevating my thoughts to think more spiritually, more humanitarianly.

The faded, white picket fence is saying my spiritual boundaries have been neglected. White is symbolic of spiritual attitudes.

The house with a picket fence around it is symbolic to me of a peaceful setting, but also the fence symbolizes setting limits and controls on oneself, such as fencing in emotions, and being under control. The faded white paint showed these things to be fading or lacking in me at the present.

The weeds and dying plants must have something to do with my relationship to my outer world. I think, "This was once a beautiful garden. All it needs is some water and care." Water is symbolic of cleansing oneself…purity of spirit, as in baptism. And care is thought, but more than thought, it is empathy. One must be empathetic with nature to have it grow into something beautiful for you. Plants are symbolic of growth, but these are dying or dormant, which says I must open up and let my nature come alive. I mustn't worry so much about the past. It can cause one to die inwardly. It's better to go forward and bring about a flourishing, a renewal of growth and vitality.

Walking up the rickety steps shows I want to venture upward, but am unsure of myself, as I am unsure of those steps. I'm afraid of falling, or losing control again, as I did with Tony. Are these the fears that I'm feeling with Bryan? Yes, that is natural. I keep putting him off when he calls. Am I just using the divorce as an excuse? Maybe I really am afraid to get involved so soon. I keep telling him I need time. Do I? Maybe I'll become a dried up old weed, like those spinster sisters.

So, in my dream, I take a chance. I venture up those rickety steps, and the porch doesn't fall in. Instead, I open the door to a beautiful scene. Opening a door is opening up to a new experience. Wow! Could it be that beautiful? The shiny wood floors show a bright new way to walk. The glowing chandelier symbolizes insight…a new awareness. The stairway is symbolic of rising to higher thinking.

The party is a celebration…an awakening. I am the girl in the white gown, in a flowing gown of purity. This is my true higher self.

The lady who said to me, "This is right," is telling me this is the way it should be, not as it was outside. Then I notice her clothes are modern. Clothes symbolize attitudes. Noticing her modern clothes might mean I need to put on more modern attitudes. Maybe she's right. Maybe I should leave the grief behind, and step into an updated new way of thinking. Maybe I should go out with Bryan. I will… if he asks me again.

Chapter 6

Into the Archives

As I drove down the dusty road to the cemetery, I found it incredible that I was actually going to all of this trouble over an old house that had no bearing on my life whatsoever. But, it wasn't just for me. Everyone I talked to seemed to be as interested in the house as I was. And they kept leading me further along in this investigation. It was sort of like trying to solve a mystery. I had always enjoyed mystery stories. It was probably that quality in my personality that led me to become a psychotherapist. In working with people, we are constantly trying to unfold the mysteries that lay hidden in the mind. Dreams help to solve those mysteries, just as the psychic, Mrs. Erickson opened new doors for us to the mystery of that old house.

The public cemetery was a mile out of town. Evidently, when it was first established, there was no church in town, so it was customary to put the cemetery on the outskirts of town. Milton never did expand enough to encompass the cemetery.

It was a narrow, gravel road. Wispy aspens lined it on both sides. Beyond the trees were fields of uncut hay. Entering the wrought iron gates of the cemetery, I saw a small, white chapel. Next to the chapel was a white bungalow, which had *OFFICE* written on its door. I parked in the chapel parking lot, and began walking among the grave markers. There was a section of the cemetery, which was obviously older, according to the age of the headstones. These marble tombstones were large and quite elaborate. Many of them were family plots.

It was easy to find the tombstone of Captain Andrew MacLean and his wife, Katherine, for it was the largest one there. An enormous wrought iron fence surrounded it. One could see he wanted all who viewed this marker to realize that he was one of the major developers in Milton. He wanted to leave his mark for posterity.

The large marble tombstone read, "In memory of Katherine Louise – Beloved and Faithful wife of Captain Andrew J. MacLean. Born in Tobermory, Scotland, the Isle of Mull on the 4th day of August 1860. Died of pneumonia in Mill Town on the 10th day of December 1889. Succeeded by her daughters, Annabelle Christine born 5 June 1883, and Elizabeth Marie born 18 May 1884." And next to Katherine's name was, "Captain Andrew J. MacLean – Sea Captain, Builder, and Lumberman. Born in Tobermory, Scotland, 10 January 1850. Died of heart failure in Mill Town 3 November 1904."

It was all there, so there was no question of whose plot of ground this was. The captain thought of everything. All that was needed for the sisters to do at the demise of the captain, was to have his death date cut into the marble marker next to Katherine's. Then, when the sisters died, two smaller markers were put near their parent's, with simply, "Annabelle Christine MacLean 5 June 1883, Milton – 1 December 1956, Milton" and "Elizabeth Marie MacLean 18 May 1884, Milton – 6 February 1957, Milton."

So Annabelle died at age 73, and Elizabeth died two months later at age 72. I wrote the dates on a small notepad I carried in my purse. Then I strode over to the small white building near the chapel. The sign on the door said, *OFFICE – Jack Jacobson, Caretaker.*

Through the door window I could see a desk, a small bookshelf, and a file cabinet, but no sign of life. I tried the doorknob, and it was unlocked. As I walked in, a bell tinkled, and a short, thin, balding man in his late eighties came out of a back room eating a sandwich.

"Howdy! What can I do fer ya?" He mumbled through his lunch.

"I live at the beach, and have become interested in the MacLean house out there on the cliff. It's for sale, and I'd like to know some more about its history."

"Well, Miss, you sure come to the right place. I've lived in Milton my whole life. And I can tell you 'bout that old house, all right."

"Did you actually know the sisters?"

"'Bout as well as anybody round these parts."

"Then, you actually talked to them?"

"Well...no...not really."

"When did you meet them?"

"When they was brung here."

"But, you said you knew them when they were alive."

"I said I knew them 'bout as well as anybody...better, in fact!"

"How can that be?" I thought he must be dimwitted or senile. I figured I wouldn't get any information from him. His face was a mass of wrinkles, and his hands gnarled like an oak tree. He was finished with his sandwich now, and had pulled out a toothpick from the pocket of his plaid flannel shirt, and began cleaning his teeth.

"Sure. Nobody really knew 'em, to associate with. They'd phone in for groceries and supplies at the store where I worked. "

"Then you talked to them when you delivered the groceries?"

"Nope. The storeowner told me to put 'em on the back porch, and knock, and leave. So I did. They never come out to thank me nor tip me, neither. I brung 'em stuff rain or shine. But it don't matter none. A couple of crazy old ladies...I never expected nuthin.'"

"And they never talked to you?"

"Nope."

"Didn't they have any servants?"

"Yup, I guess at first. There was a cook and a gardener once, but when I started delivering, they lived by themselves. I worked at the store a few years, then the town built this chapel and was lookin' fer somebody to look after it. Said I'd do it if they'd put me up a little house out here so I could be here all the time. So they built this office, with an apartment in back. I got my house paid for and all I got to do is open up the chapel for funerals, dust a little bit, and keep the files on all the residents here."

"Do you know anything more about the MacLean sisters?"

"Well, they kept to themselves. Didn't go out of that house except to tend the garden. It was a beautiful garden at one time. That was when they could still get down on their knees and tend it. Kind of went to pot near the last."

"Did anyone else live in the house?"

"After their mom died, their dad come and went, haulin' lumber by ship. I heard he wasn't 'round much when they was little. They had a cook, a housekeeper, and a gardener. The gardener lived over the old carriage house until it fell into disrepair."

"Did you ever see a cook or housekeeper on your deliveries?"

"No. They didn't need one. Don't take much to cook for two people."

"Do you remember who attended Katherine's funeral?"

"Nope, that was before my time."

"What about Annabelle?"

"Sure do. No one. We just put her in the ground. No service. Nuthin'."

"But, Elizabeth came, didn't she?"

"Nope. No one. We just put her in. That was it."

"How did she die?"

"Heart, I think. Here I'll check the records." He opened the drawer of the file cabinet, and pulled out two sheets…one on Annabelle, and one on Elizabeth. "Yep, they both died of heart. The delivery boy found Miss Elizabeth. Bob Owens, owner of the grocery store hadn't heard from her in over a week, so he sent his delivery boy over to see how she was. The boy saw the milk and bread he'd taken her a week ago still sittin' on the back porch. He went inside and found her dead on the couch… frozen stiff. Guess she just went to sleep and didn't wake up."

"Does that record tell their church affiliation?" I peered at the documents in his hands.

"Supposed to, but it don't. See, it's left blank."

"What about their parents?"

"Let me see here. Yep, says she was Scottish Episcopal. No Episcopal churches around here. Nuthin' on him, though."

"If they were Protestants, it's curious why they would leave everything to the Catholic Church."

"Yup, well, there's no Episcopal Church in town."

"But, the sisters claimed no church for their father or themselves. So, they must not have gone to church at all."

"Nope. None that I ever heard of."

"What do the nuns do out at that convent?"

"Well, it's a small convent. Only about six sisters there. They teach at the Catholic school in Milton. Some of 'em teach at the high school in Northport."

"So, they are just teachers?"

"I guess so…besides takin' care of the grounds. They've got gardens and fruit trees they tend. I've heard they sell it too. Used to be a lot more of 'em, but not many girls want to be nuns anymore. Can't blame 'em, with what they see on TV today. Everything is sex…commercials, movies and sitcoms. Kids think everybody wants it, everybody's got it, and everybody's doin' it. We're raisin' a 'I've got to have it all' generation."

"I'm sure our parents said that about us too," I smiled.

"Maybe yours. But mine was the 'kids should be seen and not heard' generation.' Kids don't know how lucky they are today!"

"Right. Anything else I should know before going out to the convent?"

"Yup. You should check out the county court house records in Northport. They tell you a lot."

"Thanks, I'll do that. And thanks for all of your help."

"Happy to oblige. If I can help you more, you know where to find me."

We parted and I headed for Northport, which was 30 miles up the coast from Milton. *Oh, well,* I thought, *nothing else to do. Might as well continue the search. At least I can bring back some information to Vivian at the museum.* I picked up a hamburger and cola at the drive-in in Milton, and devoured it on the way.

At the county court house, I searched census records on microfilm. I found that in 1900 the MacLean house contained the captain, the sisters, a cook, a gardener, a livery boy and a nurse named Sister Mary Angelica.

I also found Sister Mary Angelica was listed at the convent in the 1900 census records. Evidently, Elizabeth had a lasting illness, requiring a fulltime nurse. That is why she didn't have her coming out party.

Driving back from Northport, I decided to visit the convent and speak with the Holy Sisters. A mile from Milton, I turned up a small, paved road leading to the convent. There was nothing but tall trees and ferns on both sides of the road. It was surreal, like going into the enchanted forest in search of Snow White.

The convent was in a grassy clearing, surrounded by trees. There was an orchard, a vegetable garden, and flowering plants. A large, long, one-story cedar building dominated a few smaller utility buildings.

I walked up the steps of the large, wooden porch, which contained some chairs and small tables. A silver cross hung above the door, with Jesus dying on it. I read the sign beside the door: *The Holy Sisters of St. James Convent - "Let Your Burden Be Light".* Under the sign, hung a brass bell with a small rope to pull. I pulled the rope and it rang the bell. Soon, a face, framed in white, peered through a window panel of the wooden door. She quickly unlatched and opened the door.

"Good Day, I'm Sister Sarah."

"Hi, I'm Laura Christopher. I'm staying in a cottage on the beach for the summer, and I'm investigating the old MacLean house that's for sale out there. I was told your convent inherited furniture and a photograph album from them."

"Yes. Please come in."

It was all wood inside, with a warm and peaceful atmosphere. Sister Sarah showed me some of the elegant mahogany furniture that came from the MacLean house. Then she pointed to a large, oil portrait on the wall of a girl in her teens.

"That is Annabelle MacLean."

I looked around. "I don't see her sister here."

"No. There was no painting of Elizabeth."

"I heard there is a family album. Is there a picture of her there?"

"Yes, I believe there is. Come with me."

Sister Sarah led me to a small office with a fireplace, a lovely old wooden desk and swivel chair, surrounded by glass-faced wooden cabinets. A Tiffany lamp sat on the desk, and another Tiffany lamp stood on the floor next to a leather chair. She unlocked a wooden cabinet. "We have some of the MacLean family's personal things in here." She handed me a family album.

I sat down in the leather chair and looked through the album. Sister Sarah sat at the desk and busied herself with papers.

In the album were photos, letters and cards from relatives and friends from Scotland, England and around America. There was a wedding picture of Andrew and Katherine, and pictures of Annabelle and Elizabeth growing up. But, there were only a couple of pictures of them as adults, which had been sent to them from visitors.

"Is Sister Mary Angelica still here?"

"No, she has passed on."

"Are there any nuns here that were here when Sister Mary Angelica was a nurse at the MacLean home?"

"I don't know. Mother Bernadette has been here the longest. You can talk to her. Just a minute, I'll get her."

Sister Sarah left the room. When she returned, she was accompanied by an elderly nun in a black habit with white trim, and a soft, round, jovial face. "Mother Bernadette, this is Laura Christopher."

Mother Bernadette held out her hand to me. "Welcome, Laura. Sister Sarah told me that you are interested in the MacLean family. I hope I can be of help to you."

I shook her hand. "Thank you Sister..ah…Mother. I would like to know as much as you can tell me about the MacLean family? Did you know them?"

"No, I didn't. Sister Mary Angelica is the only one who knew them. But, she has passed on."

"Do you know why all of their estate was willed to the convent? Were they Catholic?"

"No. As far as I know, they were not Catholics."

"Did they ever attend services here or at the church in town?"

"Not that I know of."

"Why would they leave everything to the convent, then, if they weren't Catholic?"

"I imagine, because they had no relatives to leave it to. Many people leave possessions to us, because we are a charity order whose mission is to help the less fortunate."

"Yes, I can see that. Did you sell some of the furniture then?"

"No. We had a girl's school there for a few years, but then when we had to give up the house, we gave some of the furniture to the museum in town. We felt that it would benefit the county if some of the antiques were put in the museum where people could see them."

"Why did you keep the picture album and letters and personal things?"

"That was Sister Mary Angelica's wish. She was still here then. The estate was actually willed to her by the MacLean sisters."

"I found in the 1900 census that Sister Mary Angelica was residing in the MacLean home. I believe that one of the MacLean sisters was ill for a long time, and Sister Mary Angelica was their nurse."

"That seems unlikely. We are a teaching order. And we do not go into private homes, especially to nurse people back to health. The MacLean family would most likely hire a nurse from Milton. They could easily afford one."

"Would it be possible that there were two Sister Mary Angelicas living here at that time?"

"I don't believe so. Usually, if sisters have the same name, they change it in some way to prevent confusion. But, I can look in the register." She went to a wooden cabinet and pulled out a big, black book. She found the year 1900.

"Yes. There were three Mary's here, but only one Mary Angelica. Mary is a very popular name among Catholics, especially nuns," she smiled. "Other variations of Mary are Marie and Maria."

"Do you have a file on Sister Mary Angelica? Maybe something that could tell us what her connection was with the MacLean family?"

"Just a minute, I'll see." Mother Bernadette went to a wooden file cabinet and pulled out a long drawer. After shuffling through the back of it, she pulled out a small portfolio. "This is the history of Sister Mary Angelica. I can't let you have it, because it is private. But, I can tell you some of it. She was born in Detroit, Michigan, and went through school there. Well…what do you know? She studied nursing, and worked at St. John's Hospital there as a nurse. Then she came to San Francisco and entered the convent of Santa Maria there. Then she transferred to our convent and was a school nurse at the Catholic school in Milton. She had a short stay serving as a nurse in the MacLean home, the last part of 1899 and early 1900. There is a note here about the MacLean family will giving everything to her, to be dispensed as she saw fit. And here's another note signed by her that…" Mother Bernadette hesitated as she silently read the note. Then she looked up at me, with a puzzled expression.

"Yes?" I queried.

"Well…it says…that the furniture and other items from the MacLean estate are to be kept intact at this convent until called for. That's strange. We nuns take an oath of poverty. We have no material possessions to speak of. So, it has been assumed that all of the furniture belongs to the church. Maybe that's what it means, that it is all to be kept at the convent until called for by the mother church."

Then she itemized everything that was to be held in safekeeping. "Here is a post script at the bottom. It names Sister Ignatius Bennett as guardian of the estate, to succeed Sister Mary Angelica. That is very strange indeed."

"Where is Sister Ignatius? Is she here?"

"No. Sister Ignatius was transferred to the Sacred Cross Convent in San Francisco. It is kind of a retirement home for our nuns. We are so active here as teachers, that when our teachers retire, about in their seventies, they go to that convent and help as teachers and nurses for the elderly there. They can live out their lives there, still in service."

"Did Sister Mary Angelica go there too?"

"Let me see." She sifted through the record. "Yes, she did."

"So, Sister Ignatius lived here until she moved to San Francisco?"

"Yes, she's there now."

"Would I be able to speak to her if I went there?"

"Oh, yes. She is still quite active. She does historical research, and she gives workshops there. She was a history teacher in Milton."

"Thank you for your help. I appreciate the time you've given me."

"I hope it was of use to you. I wish I could have given you more information, but possibly Sister Ignatius will be able to. Good luck and God bless you on your journey." She did the sign of the cross in front of me.

"Thank you, Sister…ah…Mother." I felt good. I hadn't been blessed in, God only knows when.

I was exhilarated as I drove once more down the wooded lane from the convent. I could see why the girls wanted to become nuns. There was sanctuary and solace in that place. And both of the nuns I met were very nice. There was a peaceful reassurance about them that compels one to want to emulate them.

Chapter 7

Annabelle Comes Out, and So Does Laura

The phone rang.

"Hello?"

"Hi Laura. This is Bryan. How are you?"

"I'm fine, Bryan."

"Are you still investigating that house?"

"Yes, and I've found out some interesting things. I went to the cemetery, the county courthouse, and the convent yesterday, and talked to a nun who gave me some new information."

"I've got something to show you, too. A newspaper article about Annabelle's coming out party, which tells more about it than the paper you looked at. How about, I pick you up for dinner and we can talk about it?"

"Okay. Sounds great. What time?"

"Five o'clock okay?"

"Yes. I'll be ready. Do you know where I live?"

"Yeah, you told me you live in Larson's beach house. I know where that is."

"Okay. See you at five. Bye." I hung up the phone thinking of how easy it is to accept a date. At the time I accepted it, I wasn't really thinking of it as a date, more as collaboration on this investigation. I felt as if I were a reporter working with Bryan on a news story.

But, it really was a date…my first since the divorce. Anxiety struck… putting me where so many of my patients had been, as they spoke of their panic and immobility. Sure, they were schizophrenic, paranoid, or manic-depressive, but anxiety is anxiety, no matter *who's* wearing it. I was suddenly filled with that fearful feeling of *what will I wear, how will I look, what will I say, what will I do?* I wanted to back out of the whole situation and hide away at home.

Now, realizing I was reflecting paranoia, I started to analyze the situation. *Just because he asked me out to dinner, it doesn't mean he has any other intentions. I must consider this as more of collaboration, than a date. Yes. That will work. We will discuss the newspaper article. And I'll tell him about all of the people I talked to, and we'll decide what to do from there…I mean about the search.*

What about afterward? What if he wants to come into my house afterward to talk more? I can't just tell him no. Okay, one drink, that's all. That's sociable…maybe. It depends on how much he drinks at dinner. Coffee…I'll fix coffee for us. That's safe. The highway patrol will thank me for that. Oh, my God! I'd better clean this place up!

I scurried around picking up mail, newspapers and magazines. I dusted the living room and did the few dishes in the sink. I straightened the furniture on the deck, and decided that was where we'd have coffee. It was safe.

Then I showered and thought about what I would wear. *This will be an opportunity to wear something nice, for a change. I haven't dressed up since I've been here. But, not too dressy. I don't want him to think I'm going overboard for him. Besides, I don't think there is any place in Milton to dress up for. Blue dress, white heels and pearls. That's good enough…not too much!*

I took one last look around my living room of Early Goodwill-Late Garage Sale furniture, and decided there was nothing I could do about it. It was what it was. I heard a knock and headed for the door.

"Hi Bryan! Come in," I smiled, as I let him pass by me.

"So, this is what it looks like. Yeah, I remember that fireplace."

"Oh, you've been here before?"

"Yeah. Ed Larson lived here when he was single. He used to have some real big bashes here. Everybody brought a case of beer, and we'd keep the neighbors awake half the night. This place was so packed full of people, you couldn't see the furniture. That's why I wondered what it really looked like...without the people, I mean."

"Well, you sure didn't miss anything. This is probably the same furniture."

"Yeah." He looked around the room, and then at me. "Okay, you ready?"

"Just a minute. I'll get my coat." I pulled a lightweight white jacket from the closet.

"Good idea. It'll get cold later."

I was glad he didn't use the old cliché that he'd keep me warm.

"We're going to Northport to the Charthouse. You ever been there?"

"No, I haven't."

"Best seafood in the county. But, you can get steaks there too."

"Oh, I like seafood. It sounds great!" I led the way out the door and into Bryan's burgundy jeep. It was shiny and clean, but I wished I had jeans and tennis shoes on as I climbed up into it.

"Doesn't this thing come with a ladder?" I joked.

"I'm sorry. I should have warned you to wear pants. This jeep is the most practical thing for running around on these country roads. It's economical too. I get 17 miles to the gallon."

"That's nice," I smiled, assuming that was good mileage. The only thing I knew about my car was to keep it full of gas and windshield cleaner...and an occasional oil change.

Bryan continued, "It's got four on the floor, that'll get me anywhere."

I looked down on the floor, but didn't see four of anything, but our feet.

"That's nice," I said, with a feigned sense of awareness.

"So, tell me about your investigation, Laura."

I told him about the Catholic Church having no record of births, deaths, weddings or christenings in the MacLean name. Then I told him about the nice man at the cemetery. He laughed and said he knew Jack. He called him a funny old duffer. Then I explained the census sheets, and the fact that Sister Mary Angelica was listed both at the MacLean house, and at the convent.

"So, she didn't stay very long at the MacLean house," Bryan acknowledged. "If it had been a permanent job, she wouldn't have been claimed by the convent. They knew she was coming back."

"Yes, and I imagine the census taker thought there were two Sister Mary Angelicas."

"Yeah. They make lots of mistakes."

"I think one of the girls had a long illness, and needed a nurse. But, why wouldn't they get a nurse from Milton? Surely, they had plenty of money to afford it."

"Maybe there wasn't one available at that time. What time of year was it?"

"It was the last part of 1899, and the first part of 1900. I guess it was winter time."

"Oh, yeah, Laura. Lots of sickness in the wintertime. I could check the files for epidemics."

"Yes. That would be good. Check Northport, too. They could have sent to there for a nurse. What baffles me is, the nuns at St. James are teachers. So, why would they look there for a nurse? Maybe they knew that Sister Mary Angelica was a school nurse at the Catholic school."

"That brings up another question, Laura. What school did the girls go to? Maybe they went to the Catholic school, even though they weren't Catholic."

"Yes. Maybe that's why they called the school nurse in."

"We should check the school records, both Catholic and public to see where they went."

"Good idea, Bryan. I'll do that tomorrow."

The Charthouse sat on a large dock in the marina. Ample windows allowed people to look out at the ocean and the boats - coming, going and moored at the dock. The restaurant was designed to look like the bridge of a ship, where the captain guided the ship's course. On top of the building a flagpole stood above a crow's nest.

As we entered the restaurant, a young man, dressed in a white captain's uniform, greeted us from behind a huge ship's wheel. He carried two old-fashioned whiskey jugs, while leading us to our table. I wondered if these drinks came with our meal.

We sat down, and he handed us each a whiskey jug, saying, "This is your menu."

I looked at the whiskey jug in my hand, and saw a menu was printed on it. Soon, a waitress dressed in a sailor suit with white shorts took our order. We decided on steak and lobster for two, and chardonnay to drink.

As I glanced around the room, I saw a replica rowboat hanging from ropes in the center of the room. It was a salad bar. It was loaded with crushed ice. A huge pink shell, filled with lettuce, sat in the middle of it, while smaller shells surrounding it contained various salad items, such as mushrooms, onions, carrots, celery, cherry tomatoes and much more. Sailor waiters and waitresses bustled between shiny, spar-varnished, wooden tables. Thick resin captured pebbles, shells and pieces of ship's brass in a glittery grave of glistening color.

Bryan pulled a piece of paper out of his pocket. "This is an article I found in the Northport News June 9, 1899. It tells about Annabelle's coming out party. This reporter had a better interview than the Milton newsman. Probably because it was a woman reporter." He smiled at me with a respectful awareness of my gender, which endeared me to a greater awareness of his rugged good looks.

"The Milton paper was so small in those days," he continued, "that they probably only had one or two reporters…men. But, Northport, being the county seat, had a bigger paper. And, in keeping with the times, they had a woman reporter for the fashion section." He handed me the paper.

I looked at the article about Annabelle's coming out party. It was held in their home and 78 people attended. It described Annabelle's white gown, her hair, and satin slippers and said her father, Captain Andrew J. MacLean, presented her. It also mentioned that Annabelle's younger sister, Elizabeth would be debuting the following year, at which time both sisters would accompany their father on his ship to Europe, where they would visit many ports of interest.

"Something happened, Bryan. Elizabeth never had her party, and they may not have taken that trip to Europe, either."

"I suppose one of them got sick."

"It had to be Elizabeth. Why else would she not have her party? That was a very important thing in those days, for a girl of sixteen to be presented to society as eligible for marriage."

"The captain didn't die, did he?"

"No. I saw the death records at the cemetery. He died in the early 1900s. I have it written down at home when they all died. I also have a copy of the 1890 and 1900 census. They had the census every ten years. In 1890 they had a governess, housekeeper, cook, gardener and livery boy living there."

"Did they all live in the house?"

"I don't know. I suppose the gardener and livery boy could have lived in the carriage house, or in another building. Or if the gardener, cook and livery boy were family, they could have lived in the carriage house, and the governess and housekeeper lived inside. They certainly had enough rooms for them."

"Well, it's a cinch they all lived there, or they wouldn't have been on the census."

"Except, don't forget, Bryan, in 1900 Sister Mary Angelica was listed at both the MacLean residence and the convent. And there was no housekeeper or governess listed then."

"Yeah, well, people made mistakes in those days, too."

"Bryan, I'll bet the census takers thought there were two Sister Mary Angelicas. I thought so, too, at first."

"Could be. Are you sure there aren't?"

"Mother Bernadette assured me there weren't."

"Okay. Where to next?"

"I'll check the school records, Catholic and public school, to see if Annabelle and Elizabeth went to school at either place."

"Save yourself some footwork. Call them. They can check their records and call you back. I'm not so sure those schools were built then. You may have to call Northport School District. They may have been shipped into there."

"Speaking of being shipped, what if they were shipped off to boarding school back east, or maybe to San Francisco? How would we find that out?"

"We probably could, if we dig deep enough. But you said they had a governess. She could have taught them. Now that's a lead for you, Laura. If you really want to know, follow up with the governess. If you can find her family, they might have some information for you."

"They might, if I could find them. The governess wasn't on the 1900 census. And there was no housekeeper, just cook, livery boy, gardener and Sister Mary Angelica."

"Boy, that's strange!"

"I know, Bryan. That's why it's so intriguing to me. I just have to find out what happened."

"So...where to next?"

"I'll call the school district, but I also want to talk to Sister Ignatius, who knew Sister Mary Angelica. The MacLean estate wasn't given to the convent. It was given to Sister Mary Angelica. Of course nuns can't own any property, but there is something about it that she willed to Sister Ignatius. She lives in a retirement convent in San Francisco. I'm going to go there next."

"I'll take you. I have some business next week in Frisco. I'd be glad to have you along as company." Bryan smiled hopefully at me.

I hadn't expected that. I still didn't know him well enough to be sure I wanted to spend a whole day with him. He was nice, friendly and helpful, but I wondered if he would become possessive of me. *Why should I worry,* I thought. *I'm a big girl. All I have to do is say "no."*

"Okay. What day would you be going?" It really didn't matter to me. I had nothing else to do at the beach.

"I can go any day. What day is best for you?"

"I'll have to see. Sam Griffin was going to get that key to the attic, and we were going to take Mrs. Erickson up there, remember?"

"Oh, yeah. Be sure and call me. I want to go, too."

I looked quizzically at Bryan, deciding I wanted to know more about him. "Are you interested in psychic things, Bryan?"

He looked curiously at me, as if trying to decide whether or not he should say. "Well, sort of. I'm just curious, by nature. I guess that's what led me into newspaper work. I like to know what's going on."

"Oh, so, is this going to be one of your articles?"

"I don't know. It might. Right now, though, it's the scientist in me. I like to explore things…not just sit in the office. It's fun to get out and travel around and meet people. I'm a people person."

"Me too. But, I guess that's obvious. You don't become a psychoanalyst unless you're interested in people and the way they think. But, do you believe in haunted houses?"

Bryan laughed. "Boy, you come right to the point, don't you? Well..." He looked thoughtfully at me, as if carefully choosing his words. I could tell he cared about what I thought about what he thought. Then he answered.

"Living in a backwards area like this, people aren't afraid to speak out on what they believe. They like to gossip. That's the area pastime. The problem that most people don't have to worry about is, if it's factual or not. As a reporter, I hear a lot of stories. And...as a reporter, it's my job to report them, and not give my opinion, or try to sway the reader one way or the other. That's what I was taught by a seasoned friend, who I respect a lot. However...and there's a however to every how...after you hear so many supposedly first hand accounts of ghostly phenomenon and poltergeist activity, you begin to wonder if there isn't something to it. If you wonder enough, you'll investigate it and come up with a story. And even then, as you're writing down all the facts, you begin to doubt your own sanity. Sanity? No, not sanity, but maybe you could call it point of reference or way of looking at things."

"Yes. You can call it sanity. That's about what it is...just the way you perceive things. So, did you come to any conclusion?"

"About my sanity?" he joked.

""No, about ghosts," I grinned.

"Not really. Who really knows? It could be the spirit of the deceased just hanging around to see how things are going without him, or not knowing where to go next, or just wanting to be recognized as proof of life after death. Or, it could be left over energy that was left behind when the spirit moved on. Or maybe it's an extraterrestrial trying to get in touch with us."

"You believe in extraterrestrials?"

"Oh, yeah. We have a lot of those stories here too. I'm still on the sidelines on that one."

"Bryan, have you ever thought that apparitions might be our own mental and emotional energy manifesting in some telepathic way?"

"Sure, I've seen those movies of mediums that show ectoplasm leaving their bodies and either making things move around the room, or reconstruct in a different form. Those are just movies, but who's to say it isn't possible? Who's to say we can't move things by our thoughts? Maybe that's what's happening and we're just not aware of it."

"It sounds like you're on the sidelines of all manifestation, Bryan."

"Yeah, I guess. I'm just trying to figure out all of the angles…like a detective. I thought about being a detective when I was young. Then in college, I got on the college newspaper, then the Chicago Press, then here."

"Whatever brought you to this little town?"

"The same thing that brought you…divorce. I needed to get away from the big city and everything that reminded me of her. Something in me said, 'Go West, young man.' So I did."

"But, from Chicago to Milton? What a drastic change!"

"I needed a drastic change. My wife ran off with my best friend. We had a little girl. She was five. I love my kid, but I hate them. Couldn't look them in the eye. So I left."

"How long ago was that?"

"Six years."

"Do you write?"

"No."

"Why not?"

"My mom said they changed Debby's last name to his. That pissed the hell out of me. I wrote and told them what I thought of them. Never heard from them. I figured they wouldn't give my letters to Debby, anyway."

"She'd be eleven now?"

"Yeah. I figure I'll write a letter when she graduates from high school. I'll send her a check, and she can either use it for college, or take a trip out to see me. I'll have my mom get it to her. She knows where they live."

I knew Bryan should resolve his hatred. It isn't a good thing to live with. If he communicated with his ex-wife now, there might be the possibility of him reconnecting with his daughter. He didn't see how his anger was keeping him from his daughter, and that she would be suffering deeply, as well. But, it wasn't my place to give him advice. He hadn't asked, and I didn't know him well enough to intrude on his life. Possibly later, we would talk of it again.

For now, we talked of other things. I told him a little more about my life with Tony, the feelings of deception, remorse, anger, and ending with forgiveness. I hoped this might turn Bryan around a bit. He might see the importance of forgiving his ex-wife…even though I hadn't totally forgiven Tony.

At that time, I was still in conflict with what I knew theoretically, and what I emotionally felt. It was something that not only took time to heal, but a gradual re-education, which, unbeknownst to me, I would be led into by fate.

After dinner, Bryan drove me home. He must have been thinking about what I said about getting in touch with his daughter, because he brought it up again.

"You know, I think about Debby all the time, but I figure if I wrote, Carol wouldn't give my letters to her."

"Nothing is lost by trying. You might be surprised."

"Yeah, I miss her like hell. But I can't stand the thought of communicating with Carol and Pete. If I went back there, all that hate would well up in me and I'd probably punch him out."

"Sounds like you still love her." I gave him a quizzical look.

He frowned defiantly. "Carol? Christ no! I hate her! I hate them both!"

Me thinks thou protesteth too much, I said to myself. "Bryan, a strong emotion like hate can fester inside a person, and it prolongs feelings about that person, making it impossible to forget them. Sometimes we unconsciously set ourselves up, by clinging to an attachment, even if it is a negative one."

"Shit, Laura, that's pure crap! Maybe it's okay for your schizos, but I'm not some paranoid freak that's mooning over a bitch that ran out on him. I'm just damn mad that they were sneaking around behind my back…lying to me. What's wrong with that?"

"Nothing. I felt the same way about Tony. But then I realized it was hurting me more than it was him."

"Yeah, well, it takes time. That's why I'm waiting till Debby graduates from high school. Then she'll be old enough to fly out here to see me."

"Don't you think she'll be wondering why she never heard from you before?"

"Probably, but I'll just tell her the truth…that I didn't want to talk to her mom."

"That might not be enough, after years of rejection. You could write to Debby now, so she'll know you care about her and still love her."

"Shit, Carol would probably tear them up."

"But she might not…not if she loves Debby. She should realize what Debby is feeling now, missing her father. If you wait too long, Debby will feel that you left her because you didn't care about her."

"I didn't leave Debby. I left because I couldn't stand seeing Carol and Pete together."

"I know that, and you know that, but Debby doesn't know that. Kids always take things personally. They often think that they were the cause of parents splitting up. And her loss of you, is just as deep as your loss of her."

Bryan was silent, for a moment, as we pulled up to my beach house. He walked me to the door. I unlocked the door.

"Would you like to come in for some coffee?" I asked.

"Sure," he answered quietly. He was still melancholy from our conversation.

"It's chilly in here. Would you like to build a fire while I make the coffee?"

"Sure."

He was sitting on the couch in front of the fire, when I brought in the mugs of coffee. I sat down beside him.

"I guess you're right," he said.

"About what?"

"About me writing to Debby."

"Oh, that's good. Include your email address, so she can respond quicker."

"Yeah, I will." He sounded more hopeful now.

We talked about the house on the hill, and about Milton and the people who lived there. We laughed, and stayed as far away as we could from marital mistakes.

I walked him to the door. As I said goodbye, he leaned over to kiss me. I turned my head slightly, so we kissed cheeks. He respected that, and he squeezed my hand with a smile of sincere friendship. I was thankful that my first date was one of mutual understanding.

Chapter 8

Illusions and Allusions

It was a lazy day as I lay in the lounge chair on my deck. I attempted to read, as the sun warmed my body, and the rhythm of the waves rolling along the shore lulled me to sleep. The book fell on my face, as my mind wandered into a fantasy world of symbols and illusions.

The dream was tranquil and peaceful, reflecting my mood, as I lay serenely contented in the warm sun. *I am standing in a bedroom, which is mine, but it's not familiar to me. My sweet little white-haired grandmother is there with me. I'm so happy being there with her. I go through a door into the bathroom. I want to relieve myself, and don't want anyone to see me. So I close the door and the window. Then I am back into the bedroom, and I'm lying in the bed. Something is going on outside. There is some commotion that I'm aware of, so I can't go to sleep. I think it must be raining and dark outside. Getting up, I look out of the window over the bed, and see snowflakes falling down, softly and quietly. I know that everything is okay. I'm not to worry about outside disturbances. They will settle down like snow settles down and is quiet and peaceful. I know I'll awaken in the morning to a beautiful warm day.*

"Hard at work, I see!" A gruff, male voice startled me from my dream.

I lifted the book off my face, and stared up at the dark shadow in front of me. As my blinking eyes adjusted to the bright sunlight, I could see it was Tom standing on my deck.

"Oh, yes, I was reading. Guess I dropped off. Sit down, Tom. What brings you down the beach?"

"You."

"Oh, I'm flattered!"

"You should be. I don't walk this far for just anyone!"

"Well, thanks. I'll have to return the compliment. I've been wanting to see your place, anyway."

"It's not much." He peered in my window. "But it's a hell of a lot better than this!"

"I know. It would have to be. Anything is better than this. It's one step from sleeping in a cardboard lean-to. But it will do until summer's over."

He sat down. "Then what?"

"Oh, I'll probably go back to San Diego and resume my job at the hospital."

"You sound a bit wistful. Is that what you really want?"

"I don't know. You get spoiled lying around the beach all summer. Don't feel like doing anything after awhile."

"That's right. You've got the bug. You'd better move out while you've got an ounce of ambition left in you."

"Oh, you ought to see what I've been doing lately. I've been researching that house."

"What in the hell for?"

"Because I want to."

"Christ, Laura, you're regressing. That's a kindergarten answer."

"I know. But, it's the truth. So, it's an adult answer, as well. I really have no other reason than that it interests me. I'm not going to buy the house. But there is a mystery about it that I must solve. Something happened there and one of those sisters wants me to know about it."

"Christ, Laura, you don't believe in ghosts do you?"

"I don't know what I believe. I haven't explored deeply enough to be sure of anything."

"And then when you are sure, you still won't be sure."

I mulled that over in my mind for a moment.

"God, that's profound, Tom!"

"Thanks. Every so often I come up with a bit of profanity."

We both laughed.

"Actually, Tom, I hate to tell you this, but that is exactly what a friend told me last night."

"About how profound I was?"

"No, about thinking you know, and not really knowing."

"Life is an illusion, after all."

"Do you think so?" I asked this with intense curiosity.

"Who knows…when you think you know…" he smiled with eyebrows raised.

"You don't really know," I finished.

"Yeah, now let's get off this bullshit, and tell me who this genius was that was quoting my profanity."

"His name is Bryan Lewis. He's a reporter for the Milton Register. And he's interested in the house too."

"Is he really interested in the house? Or you?"

"A little bit of both, I think."

"Is he going to write about that house?"

"I don't know. He might. He helped me find an article from 1899 about Annabelle MacLean's coming out party. And he gave me some other leads."

"I'll bet he did!" One eyebrow flew up in devilish dismay.

"No, nothing like that. We've only had one date. Last night he took me to the Charthouse in Northport. And sometime this week we're going to San Francisco."

"Ah ha! One date and you go away for the weekend. Christ, if I knew you were that easy, I'd have made a play for you myself!"

"No, nothing like that, Tom. We're just going for the day. I'm going there to talk to a nun who should be able to tell me about the MacLean sisters, and why they kept themselves cooped up in that house."

"They were probably ugly as sin."

"No, they weren't. I saw a picture album of them at the convent. They were both pretty girls."

"Evidently, looks and money don't always win out. Now you've piqued my curiosity. I'll be interested in finding out the answer to that mystery, as well."

"Sam Griffin, the realtor, is getting the key to the attic door. Then we are going to explore it again with the medium, Mrs. Erickson. She felt something significant about the attic. Do you want to go?"

"No. I always say, let sleeping ghosts lie."

"But this one isn't sleeping. This one is troubled. And David says if we solve the problem for her, then she will be happy and move on."

"What do artists know, anyway? They spend their days sniffing oil and turpentine. You can't be sure of what they tell you."

"You sure *are* cynical, Tom."

"I know. It matches my looks."

"What do you mean by that?"

"I look in the mirror every morning, at my leathery old wrinkles and say, *you sure are an awful looking old bastard!* Then I spend the rest of the day emulating that fact."

"Tom, you aren't awful looking! Those are lines of distinction. You really look wise beyond your years."

"Like Father Time, huh? And what about the bastard part? You didn't mention that."

"I haven't known you long enough to comment on that," I winked.

He laughed. "Just hope you don't. 'Cause you'll find out I really *am* one!"

"That makes you all the more intriguing, Tom. Don't you know it's women's mission in life to find someone they can try to change?"

"Yeah, you're right. It's an unwritten law among women," he smiled.

"And pillage and conquer is the unwritten law among men."

"Yep. That's right…person, place or thing. They're all ours," he growled with possessive passion that made him look like a Viking king.

"Let's face it, Laura. You women lie around in your shorts and halter-tops, just waiting for a man to come along and notice you. Even an old fart like me will do, if no one else is available to look at you."

"For your information, I was exposing myself to the sun, not all of humanity," I retorted indignantly, as I sat upright in the lounge chair.

"Well, that proves it. The sun is masculine."

"What? Where'd you get that idea?"

"Books, Laura. All I know is what I read. In many ancient religions, the sun is the symbol for God, the creator. You can't deny that God is masculine."

"Why can't I deny it? If God is the creator, then God has the quality to reproduce. What man on earth can do that?" I felt elated in defeating the sage.

"You got me there, little lady. But, if we are made in God's image, then he is male and female."

"Yes, just as all people have the same duality," I agreed.

"Then, if we are to be perfect, as God is perfect, can we do it in this lifetime?"

"I guess there are those who have." I was hoping he wouldn't ask me who they were.

"What about the rest of us? What happens to us?"

"I guess they have different levels of existence in heaven. I'm sure they'll find a place for you, Tom. Don't worry," I grinned.

"I'm not worried about that. I'm just wondering what you know about it."

"Nobody knows anything, for sure," I mimicked him with a knowing smile.

"Right. I stand corrected, counselor. I'll rephrase it. How, do you think, one reaches perfection, if that is our ultimate goal?"

"Well, assuming that is our goal, it's quite obvious that we all won't reach it on earth. So, there must be a way we can learn to be perfect and work our way up the ranks in heaven. Maybe by helping people who are still on earth."

"Ah, visions of James Stewart in *It's a Wonderful Life,*" he grinned, with sardonic wisdom.

"Well, it's possible, Tom. Maybe we don't see them, but maybe spirit people are helping us without our knowing it. Maybe they reach us telepathically."

"That's very possible. Then when they rack up enough Brownie points, they sail on up to heaven and sit at God's feet?" he teased.

"No…not exactly…well…why not?" I was considering and reconsidering, just as he wanted me to do.

"Because, what would you do with yourself, once you became this all wonderful, so enlightened individual? Would you be satisfied sitting on a cloud and gazing into the face of God?"

"Well, no. I don't believe in a God on a cloud. I see it as more of a huge light source of power and energy and love."

"Then if you became a light source of power and energy and love, like God, would you be satisfied to float around in the atmosphere with all of the other light and power sources?"

"I don't know. If we were relieved of all of the conflicts, all of the worries, problems, and difficult relationships, and became very enlightened, knowing all there is to know, maybe we would be satisfied with that."

"So, you're saying that maybe this thirst for knowledge disappears once it is totally quenched."

"Yes, I guess so. That sounds logical, doesn't it?" I squinted at him.

"It does. But, what is the ultimate? In your belief?" He led me like a teen in his high school classroom.

"As I said, it's knowing all there is to know, and containing an all-encompassing love."

"All-encompassing means a love for the whole universe and all that it contains. Not just people. Everything. That would take a long time, wouldn't it?"

"Yes. It would."

"Then tell me, Laura, how can you develop a love for something you've never seen?"

"You mean, like God?"

"God, and all other existence. In this life, you will live in a specific area, and associate with a limited number of people, in respect to the billions of people on earth. There will be animals and plant life, which you will never know in this earthly existence. How can you grow to love, in totality, all of that?"

"I guess, with a lot of hard work in the after-life."

"Then, what is the purpose of this mere pittance of an earthly life, as compared to what lies ahead of you?"

"To get me started at it." I answered this, only half sure of myself. I felt like I was treading through quicksand.

"What if you started long before this earthly life?"

"Just what are you alluding to, Tom?"

"That you were a thinking, spiritual entity before you became a fetus in your mother's womb. Like Jesus, you were already a person, and you came to earth to accomplish something in particular."

"Where would I have come from in the first place?"

"That's right. Where did Jesus come from?"

"God created him."

"God created us too. Why did he create Jesus as a total being, and not us?"

"Maybe Jesus was his first creation. Maybe Jesus was Adam, and he decided to come back and help us."

"Then, who was Eve?" Tom smiled at me with that twinkle of wisdom and mirth.

"I don't know. Maybe Mary, his mother."

"You're not sure. But, you are thinking logically to come up with that answer. And you're doing a good job of it. Let's suppose Jesus and Mary were Adam and Eve. And they were created as perfect people to just enjoy life. But, they fell from God's graces by eating the fruit of the tree of knowledge, encouraged by the serpent, as any good Christian or Jew knows. So, they knew carnal pleasure. And they began begetting.

"Eventually, they die, still in ignorance of right from wrong, even though they had eaten from the tree of knowledge. They go to heaven and look down on how awful everyone is acting. So, they decide to help their poor sinning relatives, who are still struggling on earth. They help so much, that they work their way back into God's favor.

"In the meantime, the other wretched souls, who die on earth, come to heaven and see the good that Adam and Eve are doing. And they begin to help those on earth too. It's a nice little set up…keeps people working.

"Then, God says to Adam and Eve, "Jesus, Christ! These people are dumb! This plan is working too slowly. These guys just aren't getting the picture. Everyone is at war with their neighbors. We'll never get anywhere this way! So, he sends Adam and Eve to earth as Jesus and Mary, so they can be an example for people. And, a few more enlightened spirits come to earth to help spread the word.

"So Jesus and Mary and the disciples do their thing and go back up and sit with God. But, people on earth are still warring and sinning, except now there's a whole new industry in Bibles, crosses, statues, churches and movies. Right?"

"Well…something like that…I guess. Who really knows, anyway?"

"God only knows! But there are alternative theories, Laura."

"Like what?"

"Well, as a teacher, I had to deal with many different levels of intelligence and understanding in my students. As a shrink, you have to deal with many levels of psychosis and neurosis in your patients. We know that there are many areas of the brain that scientists haven't even delved into. Right?"

"Right."

"All people have various levels of intelligence, understanding, emotions, attitudes and maturity. These all change constantly within each individual. Right?"

"Right."

"There are many levels of awareness in life, ours being the highest. Though, sometimes I seriously doubt that fact. Scientists have found various levels of intelligence in plant life. If we believe the Bible, we accept the fact that God created all living things – air, water and earth included. To create, one must create out of what one has. Right?"

"Right."

"So, if in the beginning there was only God, then creation came from God. Everything was created out of God. Now, what common denominator have scientists found for all worldly existence?"

"Well, I guess, energy."

"Right. Everything that exists is composed of energy, including these chairs we are sitting on. Could that energy be called intelligence?"

"I don't know. I never really thought about it before."

"What is energy?"

"E=mc squared," I recited. "But, I can't tell you what that means."

"Most people don't understand Einstein's theory of relativity. It basically means that energy is made up of mass times the speed of light times itself."

"I still don't understand it."

"Well, I hardly do either, myself. But, I'll try to explain it as I see it. As we know, all things are made up of atoms. And atoms are full of energy. And energy is light vibration, which is in constant motion. And that motion sends out a terrific radiation of light energy, which is basically what we are. Every place and space of our bodies is filled with light energy. All of our organs, tissues, fluids, muscles, bones, hair, teeth and nails are filled with atoms of light energy vibrating at different intensities.

"Scientists have calculated the number of atoms in an average person's body, and figured the energy contained in it. And they have found that we humans have tens of thousands times more energy than an atom bomb."

"That's incredible!" I exclaimed.

"I know. It is. And you are incredible. I'm incredible. Everyone is incredible. We are all wonderful, powerful masses of incredibly intelligent energy. And we have the power to create what we want in our lives… by our thoughts, our beliefs and our actions. In fact, *we are* creating our life by our thoughts, beliefs and actions. The trouble is, most of our thoughts, beliefs and actions are negative. So our life turns out negative, or contrary to what we want it to be."

"Yes, I've told my clients that if they can change their thoughts, their lives can change for the better."

"Right! If we change our thoughts, beliefs and actions from the negative to the positive, then our life starts changing, and good things come to us. People and opportunities come into our lives, making us happier and more successful in all that we do."

"And isn't that the purpose of life…to be happy and successful?" I asked.

"I would say so. When we are successful in what we do, and we are doing what we like, then we are happy. And when we're happy, we want to help others to be happy."

"That's right." I smiled. "And when we do things for others, out of love and respect, then it makes us happier, and gives us a new purpose in life."

"And that includes a respect for all life. Laura, if everything has its own level of energy, or life, or intelligence, then there is a purpose in life for all living things. We should have respect for all of life; even the lowest forms of existence, because it was created on this earth for a purpose. If we believe in a hierarchy of intelligence from the lowest of plant life and beyond, to who knows where, to human intelligence, and who knows where it peaks, then we must recognize that there is an Infinite Intelligence that is the source of all life.

"Possibly the one great purpose in all of life is growth. And, possibly, that purpose is not finite. It might be an infinite master plan, that continues to recycle."

I listened incredulously. Then I burst out, as I realized what he might be intimating. "Tom, you're not telling me that you believe in reincarnation, are you?"

"What is reincarnation?" He asked this as if we were sitting in an ashram in India.

"Look, Tom, this is not a classroom. I'm not one of your high school students that you can lead and cajole into a corner."

"Oh, really?" He grinned, knowing full well I was wrong. He could lead me by the nose with the arch of his eyebrow. And I would follow along like a hungry puppy.

"Listen," I sat upright and stated emphatically, "I'm not entirely ignorant of the Bible, nor of Eastern religions either. In fact, I've been to a lot of different churches. My parents didn't go to church.

As a surgeon, my father worked on Sundays. So, growing up, I went to church with my friends. I've been to everything from the Jewish Temple to the Quakers."

"Good! And what did you learn from all of that?"

"That we all want the same thing - peace and love."

"Right! Where do you get that?"

"Well, you have to work on it to get it. You have to work on yourself and on your relationships with others."

"That's right, Laura. But a lot of people think you have to bow down and bargain with a deity in the sky to get what you want."

"So, how does all of this relate to reincarnation?"

"We talked about the many different levels of intelligence, understanding and emotional stability. Now, we are talking about the many levels of spiritual awareness. Since you've gone to so many different churches, you've probably found different levels of spirituality in the people of those different churches?"

"Yes, I have."

"When you see a person defy all religious teachings, you don't condemn his church for it, do you?"

"No, of course not."

"And likewise, when you find one saintly person in a church, you don't assume that everyone there is a saint, do you?"

"Of course not."

"Then, we must recognize that there is an individual spiritual hierarchy, as well."

"I doubt that anyone would refute that."

"So," he continued, "is that spiritual hierarchy just among humans or does it refer to the animal kingdom, as well?"

"I really don't know, Tom. I know people who swear that they can communicate with their dog or cat. Maybe there is a sense of conscience in animals. Have you ever noticed how a dog will act ashamed when you scold him?"

"Yes, it's possible that animals have a conscience. After all, what *is* right from wrong? Doesn't it have to be taught? A dog craps on the floor and gets scolded for it. Then he sulks off into a corner by himself. Next time he goes to the door, so he doesn't make the same mistake. A tot takes off his diaper and poops on the floor. His mom spanks him for it, and sits him on the pot. He cries and feels badly, but eventually he goes to the pot instead of the floor."

"But that's conditioned response…learned behavior," I interrupted.

"If there is no conscience, can it be learned?"

"Well, there has to be *some* degree of intelligence."

"But, what about conscience? Conscience isn't the same as intelligence is it?"

"Good question, Tom. The sociopath has no sense of conscience. He doesn't care what he does to others. However, he might have any degree of intelligence."

"Then, that spark of something that makes an animal sulk away is his conscience, which wants approval and respect?"

"Yes, I guess so."

"The animal and the child must learn right from wrong to live in a household. If they both lived out in the woods, what would they need to know?"

"Survival techniques."

"Would they need to have a conscience?"

"Sure, at least the boy would."

"But, out there they could both take a crap anywhere they wanted to. There would be no one to reprimand them for anything."

"Yes, but, they would set up a natural hierarchy among themselves and the other animals, and establish and maintain their own rules. It is proven that animals do this."

"That's true, Laura. So, now you could see the dog sulking off when the boy reprimanded him? Or the puppies cowering when the bitch smacked them for nursing too much."

"Yes, but what does this have to do with reincarnation?"

"I'm not saying that animals believe in a higher power, and strive to attain it. Though, who knows? Maybe a dog *does* think, *By God, next time, I'm coming back as a man, so I can deck that son-of-a-bitch that keeps kicking me!* But, if we just concentrate on the spiritual development of humans, it seems a natural way to attain perfection, through successive lives and experiences."

"Why?"

"Because, if you want to be perfect in every way, you can't love the underdog, without having known shame and rejection. You can't really empathize with the blind, crippled or maimed without undergoing some sort of sensitizing experience. As you know, feelings are not things that can be verbally taught. Feelings are learned responses to external stimuli."

"Stemming from a desire to be loved," I added.

"Yes. The two greatest commandments are based on love. Love God…Good with all of your heart, mind and soul. And love thy neighbor as thy self. On these, all the rest are based."

"So true, Tom. And most people, who try to love their neighbor, forget to love themselves. You have to be able to see the love in yourself, before you can truly see it in others. I've told many patients that, but in different words, of course."

"Yeah, and it takes a lot of trial and error before you can see the love in others. The baby comes into this world strictly out for what he can get – food and attention. Some people don't change that much."

"I know. That's why they make babies so cute and cuddly, so they'll attract our attention. It's strictly a means of survival."

"There's more to it than just survival, Laura. If we say that our life's purpose is to reach perfection, then we're going about it backwards."

"What do you mean?"

"Well, there's nothing more perfect than a baby. They're beautiful, innocent, untouched by prejudice and hate. Dumb, but perfect otherwise."

"Right, Tom. Then we ruin it by teaching them to hate, destroy, be selfish, demanding…"

"Wait a minute, little lady. Maybe we don't teach it. Maybe they already knew it, but it was temporarily forgotten."

"I don't understand. How could that be?"

"Okay, I'm going clear back to Adam and Eve again. Suppose when creation took place, it took place simultaneously throughout the world. There were many Adams and Eves. It could be literal, as in the Bible. Or it could have been evolutionary…a gradual evolvement. I'm not going to get into that. I'm just supposing that these beings walked the earth, and ruled the animals and vegetation. They warred against each other for property and power. Then they slipped off their mortal shell. This put them on the spiritual plane, where they couldn't war or own anything. They just sat around watching how stupid people on earth were acting, and wished they could do it over again, and get it right.

"Realizing their mistakes, they felt the need to incarnate again, to prove that they could do better. However, you can't prove you know it, if you've got the answers to the test in front of you. So, they take away the notes. This is not an open book test. And you come back into this world, unsure, ignorant and innocent. But, as you grow, there are tendencies and flashes of memory, which keep intruding on your consciousness. I don't know all about the conscious and subconscious, like you do. So I can't be specific about how this works."

"No one knows for sure how the brain works. We just do the best we can with what we know."

"And that could change tomorrow." He gave me a raised eyebrow and a smile.

"So true!"

"Anyway, I'll tell you how I think it's set up," he continued. "I think that your conscious mind, is the part that is aware of things around you."

"That's right."

"And your subconscious is like the memory part of you…the things you have forgotten, but are still there, stashed away, for when you might need them."

"Yes, and the things you have repressed, too."

"But, not just in this life, but in past lives, too."

"Why does it have to be past lives?"

"Because, we all have different talents, interests, goals and abilities. And those things start appearing early in life."

"I agree, but what about genetics?"

"There are kids who are terrifically talented, such as playing instruments, but whose parents can't carry a tune in a paper bag. And they don't play anything but the radio."

"Maybe their parents encouraged them with lessons."

"Then why can one kid in a family become a child protégé, and another have no talent at all on any instrument?"

"Position in the sibling lineup, favoritism, or emulating someone else."

"How about Mozart? His sister was a musician, and did fine. But little Amadeus sat upon the piano stool at age four, and played note for note what his sister had been playing. He did this without a lesson. And, when he was five, he played his own compositions for royalty. Later, as a conductor, he knew every note of every instrument in the score.

"Toscanini did this, as well. He had a photographic memory. He studied the score in one night. Then, the next day, he conducted a full orchestra, and could hear one wrong note played by a musician, and correct him, telling him which page and line it was on, without ever looking at his music. This is musical genius that very few people have."

"They must have been encouraged by family or teachers," I persisted.

"Beethoven wasn't allowed to touch his brother's music. His brother locked it up from him. Late at night, when everyone was asleep, young Beethoven would steal his brother's music, and sneak into the attic and copy the music, so he could teach it to himself. There was something more, compelling these boys toward musical genius. They had found a talent and love for music, way before they rediscovered it as children."

"I still say, there must be another answer to child genius. I still don't see why we have to come back."

"Why did we come here in the first place, Laura?"

"Because, God sent us."

"Why did God send us here?"

"Because he wanted to."

"Oh, he had nothing better to do up there in the sky, so, just for fun, he made a bunch of people, animals and plants to entertain him."

"Well, why not?"

"Okay, why not? Something to do for entertainment...sit up there and watch what stupid asses we can make of ourselves. Laura, look at the way flowers grow, die and reseed themselves...all by themselves, or with God's help, if you wish. Watch the sun rising and setting, the tides, the solar system, and even a baby being born. There is an incredible perfection to this earth. Nothing is by chance. It all falls into place beautifully. And there is purpose to it all. The ant knows what his job in life is, as does the honeybee, whether queen, worker or drone. That means, if there is a purpose for all of this other life on earth, then there must be a perfect plan for us."

"I'm not denying that. I'm just saying, I'd hate the thought of having to come back and go through the heartache I've already gone through. I want to get this over with, and go on to something better."

"You do, but not in the way you're alluding to. You are assuming that, with death, you'll automatically be in a beautiful heaven."

"Sure. Why not? There are a lot of cases of people being in a coma, or near death, and coming back and telling about the beautiful experience they had. They felt as though they were in heaven. And they didn't want to come back. In fact, these people were in a prolonged state of depression when they came back to the reality of life on earth."

"Yeah, Laura, I've read about them too. And maybe they had those experiences so they could come back and tell about life after death. It's similar to Jesus coming and telling people what to look forward to."

"Or, it all could be an illusion, Tom." I smiled at him, returning his own material.

But, as usual, he got me back, by asking, "How could it be an illusion?"

"Well, as you know, the mind can play many tricks on us. We can hallucinate without the use of drugs – see a mirage in the desert, and believe it; think we are experiencing something we've experienced before…deja vu; or have a clairvoyant experience. There are all kinds of ways the mind hallucinates, even when we are asleep."

"I've often wondered about that, Laura. How do you know when your dream really means something, or when it's just a fantasy or hallucination?"

"Well," I gave him my most profound look. "You know it really means something to you, if it really means something to you."

"Christ, Laura, now you sound like me!"

"I guess it's rubbing off," I laughed. "Okay, seriously, there *are* hallucinating dreams. Anyway, that's what is presently thought in the field of psychology. But, as you know, that could change tomorrow. We don't know everything about the mind, and we could even be wrong about that. But, it is thought that we have dreams, which are brought on by indigestion or illness, which is the mind just playing around, fantasizing. The brain never sleeps, it just keeps chugging along responding to various bodily stimuli."

"Like when you have to go to the bathroom at night?"

"Yes, but we often incorporate that into our dream, by looking for a bathroom."

"So, if we're looking for a bathroom in our dream, it just means we really have to go?"

"Not necessarily. It can also mean that you need to release something mentally, which has been bothering you."

"So, how do you know which it is?"

"By writing your dream down, and seeing what it means to you. You see, when we are sleeping, the brain isn't over stimulated with daily activities. It is more relaxed without the conscious mind bombarding it with worries, frustrations and daily anxieties. So the subconscious mind can bring out visions of the past, and show in picture form, what the problem is, how we are dealing with it, and what we could do about it."

"Wow! I didn't know you could get all of that from your dreams!"

"Yes, that's the purpose of dreams…to help us better understand what we are going through, and how to handle it better. In dreams, the subconscious brings out problems we haven't been able to solve, and things we have suppressed and repressed. It is still primitive, in the sense that it can't type out a memo for us to read, so it makes pictures for us, like the cave dwellers did for their descendants.

"If you've been hateful and mean to someone, your dream might make a picture of you being hateful and mean to that person, so you could see yourself. But that wouldn't work, because you would deny it, just as you have been doing all along, stubbornly contending that you were right and the other person was wrong."

"Yeah, that's human nature. No one wants to admit they're wrong. We're all such selfish bastards. Such honorable lineage, to be made in God's image," Tom recited with an air of sarcasm.

I continued. "So, your mind builds pictures, which fascinate, startle, and scare you, in order to capture your full attention to the severity of the problem. You have a nightmare of being chased by an evil form, sometimes just a dark form, and sometimes an ugly, terrifying creature. It depends on how seriously you take yourself. You wake up scared, remembering the dream vividly. You needed to be scared into realizing how ugly you have been behaving."

"But, how do you know it's *you* you're being chased by, and not your stomach?"

"You usually don't know, unless you write your dream down. In writing it out, the answers come to you.

"Then, if I don't write it down, the whole purpose of the dream is lost," Tom conjectured.

"Not really. The purpose of the dream was to bring into consciousness what you have been repressing. And it did just that. And, even if you don't write it down, it will be in the recesses of your mind, until it eventually dawns on you, in some way, and a new understanding is revealed. But, this might take quite a while. In the meantime, you'll go on making the same mistakes. That's why it's important to write down your dreams, and analyze them."

"How can I analyze them? I don't know enough about it."

"You've studied Greek mythology. You've read extensively. You are a master of metaphors. Dreams are universal symbols, which we all subconsciously know. For instance, what does a car mean to you?"

"It means transportation."

"So, you dream you are driving a car down a bumpy road. Suddenly, there's a roadblock. You get out of the car, and look around. What does this mean to you?"

"I'm going somewhere, but not too fast, because it's bumpy. And I'm stopped. So I look around to figure out what to do."

"That's right. You are driving yourself. This means you are in control of your life. But it's bumpy, showing that things are a little difficult for you. The way you are going is not as smooth as you would like it to be. Your dream says to stop and take a look around you. Maybe there is a different way you should be going."

"Yeah, I see. That really is easy."

"Yes, it is. Sometimes they are a bit harder to figure out, but the main thing is to ask yourself what each part of the dream means to you. Sometimes you have to pick out each symbol, and relate it to you personally. I just remembered the dream I was having when you woke me up.

"I was standing in a bedroom. A house in your dream is you. A bedroom, to me, means a place to go to rest."

"Or it could mean something else…to me." Tom smiled with a cognizant eyebrow.

"True. But this is my dream. So, the purpose of it is to put my mind at rest.

"I see my sweet, little, old white-haired grandmother, who has passed on. I'm so happy to see her and be with her. But I feel the need to relieve myself. I go into the bathroom. Now, this doesn't mean literally going to the toilet. Symbolically, it means to relieve myself of the problem that has been bothering me. This is the grief and guilt of not being able to make my marriage work, and from Tony's leaving me for other women.

"I don't want anyone to see me. So I close the door and the window in the bathroom. Just as in literature, the eyes are the windows of the soul. So I'm closing my eyes, or my mind. In other words, I'm suppressing what I don't want to see. The door is symbolic of an opportunity, like an open and shut case, metaphorically speaking. Closing the door is closing out the opportunity for growth. In other words, if you try to repress anger, rejection, hate or other emotions, which are a natural release, like going to the bathroom, you close the door on your opportunity to grow and understand yourself."

"Yeah, I know what you mean. When my wife died, I bottled up all of my emotions, and didn't want to talk to anyone about it."

"That's a natural tendency, Tom. We all have it. We feel vulnerable. So, we hide our feelings, so people can't keep opening up the wound. Repressing is bottling up inside of us what we don't want to look at. It's like closing your doors and windows.

"My grandmother, in the dream, symbolizes to me, the wonderfully happy marriage she had…reminding me of the guilt I'm harboring, in not being able to make my marriage work.

"So, then I am back into the bedroom, and I'm lying in the bed. This means I want rest and peace of mind. *But, something is going on outside. There is some commotion that I'm aware of, so I can't go to sleep. I think it must be raining and dark outside.* This means, although I want peace of mind within, I'm still aware of the conflict and turmoil I'm consciously having about letting go.

"I get up and I look out of the window over the bed. And, I see snowflakes falling down, softly and quietly. I know that everything is okay. I'm not to worry about outside disturbances. They will settle down like snow settles down and is quiet and peaceful. I know I'll awaken in the morning to a beautiful warm day.

"This means I need to get up and open my eyes…the window… to a new realization. And the realization is that when I release these feelings, what was a conflict in me, will turn into something as peaceful as snowflakes falling down."

"That's really something, Laura. But how do you know you aren't dreaming about a house because you are concerned, right now, about where to live? And you go into the bathroom because you really have to physically go? And you dream you're in bed because you're tired? And you dreamed about snow because a cool breeze just blew by and chilled you?"

"That all may be very true. Your physical condition can trigger your dream images. I have dreamed I had to go potty, and awakened needing to go. I'm sure we all have. But, who's to say we didn't wake up needing to go potty because we were dreaming about the need for a total release in our own psyche?"

"Okay, you said that some dreams are hallucinogenic. Then how do you know this one wasn't?"

"As I told you before, because it has meaning for me. Also, because I've been studying my dreams for quite a few years, and I can see a pattern in them. The dream begins by telling what the purpose of it is. In this case, the bathroom shows the need for release. Then it shows me what I'm doing. Here I'm closing the door to opportunity and the windows of my mind. Then it shows me what I should do about it, represented by getting up, opening the window and looking out to the peaceful snowflakes and beauty in life."

"And what was your grandmother there for?"

"I think about all of the things that she represents to me. I loved my grandmother dearly, and felt very sad when she died. But, she was very old and sick, and I had to accept that she must go on to a new life. That whole statement can be very significant and symbolic of my present situation…releasing the past and going on in a new mode. But, she can also represent the idea of going into this dream bedroom to look for peace and rest, because I always felt very peaceful and restful in her presence. But then, if you get into the Greek mythological archetypes, such as Freud and Jung used in dream interpretation, people in our dreams symbolize the different levels of our psyche, such as, the mother, father, child, hero and other parts of us. In that respect, she would symbolize the wise old person whom I should listen to…my higher consciousness, or conscience.

"When someone with authority is in your dream, like a doctor, teacher or older, wiser person, they are there to remind you that this is important and you should listen. Now, I can use any or all of those interpretations, because they are all valid and significant. The more we study our dreams, the more we will see in them."

"Have you ever heard of an out-of-body experience?" Tom asked.

"Yes. I've read of it. That is what's believed to be happening to people when they have near death experiences. They usually float above their physical body, and watch it being operated on. Then, they float higher and feel like they're in heaven."

"Right. And they often see passed on loved ones."

"Yes, often the passed on entity talks to them and tells them they have to go back."

"Then, how do you know you weren't actually visiting your grandma, instead of just dreaming about it?"

"How does the comatose patient know that he isn't dreaming, instead of visiting a discarnate relative?"

"Good question, little lady. I suppose, by the feeling they have when they wake up."

"Yes. And that's how I know, as well."

"But, do you really know?" he persisted.

"Does anyone?" I replied.

"As I said, life is an illusion," said my wise, old sage.

"I guess I'll have to agree with you there," I smiled.

Chapter 9

San Francisco, Open Your Golden Gates

The alarm clock on my cell phone shattered the tranquil morning air. I groped for the switch, and wondered why, though my eyes were open, I saw nothing. I pulled my phone to my face. Its iridescent numbers read 4:30 am. I lay in bed contemplating why I had agreed to go so early with Bryan. It seemed like a good idea at the time, but now I wished I had told him I'd go by myself. Getting up at 4:30 while on vacation is insane! But I did it. I knew if I lay there any longer, I'd be back asleep. So, I got out of bed, and stumbled to the bathroom.

Bryan had a 9 am appointment in San Francisco. It took two hours to get there, and an extra hour for getting hung up in the morning city commute. Moving slowly this early in the morning, I needed a full hour to get ready. I decided to wear brown slacks, a beige blouse, with brown blazer and pumps. I had heard that San Franciscans were dressier than San Diegans. Besides, I needed slacks to get in and out of Bryan's jeep.

I was thankful that Bryan was used to such ungodly hours, for he had brought along a thermos of coffee, two mugs and a box of donuts. I clung gratefully to the mug of coffee, balancing it in the air, as it swished in rhythm to the bumps in the road. This was more coordination than I was used to so early in the morning.

Bryan sensed that I wasn't an early riser, so he didn't ask me questions. He chattered about everything he could think of, as we started out. By the time we reached San Francisco, I knew his life story, all about Frisco, and the man he was meeting at the Chronicle. His pre-dawn hyperactivity was far beyond any stimulation that might be aroused in me. But now, I was okay; I was full of caffeine, calories and conversation as we pulled up to the Chronicle.

"I won't be long," Bryan said. "Ted has to catch a plane by ten, then I'll show you around Frisco, and after lunch we'll go out to the convent. Do you want to come in with me?"

"No, I think I'll wait here. I brought a book to read." I preferred the quiet of the car to a noisy newspaper building.

After Bryan's meeting, he drove me around San Francisco, pointing out the sights and telling me the history of the town. We had lunch at Fisherman's Wharf. Then, we drove out to the convent.

The convent was situated on a hill overlooking the city of San Francisco, with its bay of ships and sailboats, and its magnificent bridges spanning from knoll to knoll. The convent sat on several blocks of Catholic real estate. There was a church, a rectory, a school, a convent and lovely gardens…all of them, very old. It was quite impressive. Wide, green lawns spread out to neatly groomed hedges, flowerbeds, bushes and a variety of trees. There were fountains, gravel paths, benches and meditation nooks.

All of the buildings were early California stucco, with red tile roofs, except the convent rest home. It was an old three-storied Victorian Mansion, which had been left to the church by a prominent Catholic family. A one-storied structure, with additional rooms, had been added on to the back of the main house. I imagined this was for those in wheelchairs.

A sister greeted us at the door of the mansion, and led us into an early 19th century parlor. As we waited in the stately silence, I whispered to Bryan, "They must have no trouble getting these furnishings, with people leaving whole estates to them."

"Yeah," he whispered back. "I suppose the little, old nuns like it, too."

"If most of the convents are furnished with old things, like the one in Milton, they would feel right at home here."

"No," came from the lips of a sweetly serene face, smiling out from black and white. "They all aren't this old. Some of our convents are very modern. Good afternoon. I'm Sister Ignatius." She offered her hand to Bryan and me. As I held her hand, her warm congeniality moved from my palm, up my arm and through my body. I was immediately at peace.

We introduced ourselves, and Sister Ignatius led us out to a porch, where we could see the city far below bustling in animated urgency.

"We can enjoy the view, as we talk. I like to take my afternoon tea here. The flowers are so glorious. And you can see the sailboats on the bay. Would you like coffee, tea or a cold drink?"

"We just finished lunch," I said. "But, a cold drink would be nice."

"Okay, how about iced tea?"

"That sounds great! Thank you."

Sister Ignatius peeked in the double French doors, and asked someone to bring iced tea to us. Then she sat with us in high-backed, white, wicker chairs near a small table on the porch. She told us the history of the mansion, and she pointed out several other large homes within view, which were owned by wealthy families, many who were Catholic.

"That is why we have this wonderful spot to sit on," she smiled. I didn't know if she meant the nuns, or the three of us sitting on the porch. I loved the feeling of the elegant opulence of the Victorian Age. *I would have enjoyed living in that era,* I thought. *Maybe I did,* I chuckled inwardly, thinking of Tom and his notion of reincarnation.

"It takes you back, doesn't it?" Sister Ignatius smiled at me. She must have noticed the wistful look on my face. For a moment, I was startled by her words, intimating a past life experience. "The tranquility of this environment brings out the romance of a by gone era in most of us," she added.

"Why, Sister, you should be a writer!" Bryan exclaimed.

"I am, of sorts," she replied humbly.

"Have you published anything?" He asked.

"No. I haven't. But, I am working on a history of this house and its adjacent neighborhood."

"My, that is a big undertaking, Sister," I replied.

"Well, I'm not telling the history of each family in the area. It is more of an anthology of the Catholics settling here, and developing this religious community."

"That's great, Sister!" said Bryan. "My newspaper could print a series of articles, if you would let us."

"Oh, I don't know if the rest of the world is as interested in old houses as I am." Sister's look was one of serious humility.

"We are!" Bryan and I chorused. We all laughed.

"Sister," I began, "what do you know about the MacLean house?"

"Oh, quite a bit. That is where I became interested in old houses."

"How is that?" Bryan asked.

"When the MacLean house was given to the convent, I was just a young novice, and Sister Angelica asked me to be one of the nuns who kept it going. She knew my love for gardening, and felt that I could help the other nuns learn to appreciate it. You see, it fell into considerable disrepair toward the end when the MacLean sisters had it. They were getting too old to maintain it, and they chose not to hire a gardener. By then, their funds were running low."

"Why did they give it to the church?" Bryan asked the question I had wanted to ask for a long time.

"There were several reasons. They had no relatives to leave it to. They knew that we could use it and would take good care of it. They knew that we were in a position to bring it back to where it was and wouldn't be likely to tear it down. And they had a high regard for Sister Mary Angelica."

"Were they Catholic?" I asked.

"No. They weren't Catholic." Sister looked solemn.

"Did they go to the Catholic School?" Bryan asked.

"No, they didn't. They had a governess, who taught them until they were teenagers."

"Then what?" Bryan asked.

"They no longer needed the governess, so she sought other employment."

"Possibly they had grown beyond her level of instruction," I surmised.

"Possibly," Sister agreed.

"Did they go away to high school or college?" Bryan asked.

"No, they didn't." Sister Ignatius looked sad.

I sensed there was more. "Sister, what happened?"

"Laura, when you phoned, I had to make a decision. I prayed that I would know what to tell you. And now, after talking to you, and getting to know you both, I have decided. I will tell you."

I leaned back contentedly, on the over-stuffed cushion, and listened intently as she spoke.

"As you know, the estate was left to Sister Mary Angelica. She was in charge of it. And she made it a convent school for girls. Then when she was nearing the end of her life here on earth, she made me guardian of the estate…that is, what was left after the house was sold.

"She told me that someday someone would come and ask about it. And I would know, at that time, whether or not to pass the story on to them. And, if no one came during my lifetime, I was to pass the story on to one of the younger sisters. Sister Mary Angelica has written the story, and it is in my personal file, to be read at my death, and to be passed on.

"But, meeting you two young people, I feel that it is time for the story to be told. Even though you are a newspaperman, Bryan, I can see a sensitivity in your eyes, which I feel I can trust."

"Yes, Sister. I'm Catholic, and I would never forsake my church for a story."

"Well, there may be something that you can do…but let me tell you the story first."

We both nodded our heads, smiling in appreciation. And Sister Ignatius continued.

"Captain Andrew John MacLean was from the Isle of Mull in Scotland. I had an opportunity to go to Scotland one year with a member of my family, and we visited the Isle of Mull. I wanted to see what it was that made the Captain such a hard man. And I found out. You see, as a history teacher, I have always been interested in the origins of things. Just as you two are.

"By ferry is the only way that you can get to the island. It is very remote and almost solid rock. So, the main sources of income there are raising sheep and fishing. The sheep can traverse the rocky cliffs, and survive on the grasses there. Regardless of the rock, it is very green and very lovely. The towns are small, and the roads are barely adequate for two cars to pass. But, there are some lovely castles, which are owned by the MacLean clan.

"You see, during the time of the clans in Scotland, various areas were owned by different clans, and there was constant fighting over property rights. The MacLean's owned the whole island. And they maintained a living by preying upon ships that passed by the island. This was before sheep had been brought to the island.

"It may sound like I'm digressing. But, having seen this island, and what a hardship it was to live there, I can see why Andrew MacLean went to sea. And why he was such a hard and unforgiving man. The environment that he came from was hard and unforgiving. Maybe that's what made him such a successful sea captain. One couldn't be soft in that occupation.

"Captain MacLean had sailed into San Francisco Bay many times, moving cargo to and from the British Isles, Europe and America. He saw the lumber industry growing, and all of the money that was being made here. So, he explored the areas north of San Francisco, which hadn't yet been touched. And he bought a lot of land there, and began a lumber company. He had docks put in to take the lumber out in ships, because the railroad didn't go that far at that time.

"He had a big, beautiful, Victorian house built on the cliff for his new bride, Katherine, whom he married and brought over from Scotland. They had only two daughters, Annabelle and Elizabeth, who were six and five when their mother died. I can't remember the date, just now, but it's all in Sister Mary Angelica's letter.

"The girls were reared by a governess and housekeeper, who lived in the house. Then there was a cook, who was married to the gardener, and they had a boy who helped with the horse and carriage. They lived above the carriage house. You'll find out later why I'm telling you all of this." We nodded in appreciation.

"After Katherine's death, Captain MacLean came home as often as he could, to see his girls. But, that wasn't often enough. The girls lacked supervision, the kind that a mother and father could give them.

"When Annabelle turned sixteen, the governess arranged a coming-out party for her. It was held at the mansion, and the captain was there. He announced that the next summer, right after Elizabeth's coming-out party, the girls would sail with him to Europe, for a grand tour of Europe and the British Isles.

"The captain's gift to Annabelle was a full-sized portrait of her, which he had commissioned to be painted by a young, American artist named Simon Doran. It hung over the fireplace in the parlor at that time. The captain had also commissioned another portrait to be done of Elizabeth, for her sixteenth birthday. He had Simon stay in town, the summer after Annabelle's party, so he could paint Elizabeth's portrait while he was there. Then, when it was finished, the two portraits would hang above the two fireplaces in the ballroom, where mirrors hung at that time."

"Yes," I said. "I saw Annabelle's picture at the convent. It is lovely. But, what happened to Elizabeth's?"

"I'll get to that in a moment. Later, when Sister Mary Angelica was living with the MacLean sisters, they told her that their father was very proud of living in America. That is why he chose an American artist to do the paintings. However, the captain should have chosen an older artist, for as the artist was painting Elizabeth, she was falling in love with him. The young artist had lodgings in Milton, paid for by the captain, so he rode a horse to the house each day and sometimes at night. Somehow, Elizabeth and Simon would sneak away, without anyone knowing about it. And Elizabeth conceived.

"She didn't tell anyone for quite a while, because she wanted the portrait finished. She knew her father wouldn't allow her, at age fifteen, to marry Simon, leastwise, to a penniless artist, no matter how good a painter he was. She was sure her father would send her lover away, as soon as he heard of it. So, she kept her secret from them all, until the portrait was finished. Then, she thought she could convince her father to let them marry and live off of her inheritance until Simon became successful. But, she was wrong. She underestimated the temper of a Scotsman.

"Going behind his back was a cardinal sin, according to his belief. And the night she told him of their deception and her condition, both the portrait and the artist disappeared. The next day, the governess was fired for not watching them more closely. The captain shipped her back to her family on the East Coast.

"When Elizabeth asked him about the boy, the captain said that his name would never be mentioned in that house again. He said no one would know about the pregnancy. He would find a nurse to stay with the girls, who would not tell anyone about it.

"The captain felt that he couldn't trust anyone from town, so he went to the convent, and offered a large sum of money to have someone come and take care of Elizabeth during her pregnancy and a while after it."

"Weren't they afraid the housekeeper or cook would tell someone in town?" I asked.

"Well, unfortunately, the wrath of the Scotsman fell upon the housekeeper, too. She was fired, because she was living in the house and was supposed to be responsible for the girls, as well. So, the housekeeper was shipped to the Midwest, where her family lived."

"What about the cook and gardener and their son?"

"They were living in the carriage house. They were told that if any of this got out, that they would be out of there, too. They knew not to tell, or the three of them would be out with no home and no job.

"So, then it was the captain, the two sisters and Sister Mary Angelica living in the house. The boy drove Sister Mary Angelica to the convent every Sunday for chapel service. If anyone asked them why Sister Mary Angelica was living there, they were told that she was tutoring the girls, which was the truth. Sister Mary Angelica coached Elizabeth on maternity care, and she also instructed both girls in housekeeping and cooking.

"You see, the captain had told Elizabeth that she had brought such shame upon the house, that no one would be permitted to enter it again. They were told that they would do all of the household chores from then on. He said they needed, not only punishment, but discipline and to be kept busy.

"The captain spent the winter months home, and saw to this commandment. The baby was born the middle of March in...1900...I believe. It was a girl. Elizabeth wanted her to be named Mary Angelica, because they loved Sister so much. She had become like a mother to them, even though Sister was in her twenties. But the captain put his foot down. He said Elizabeth would not be allowed to name the baby, and he packed up Sister Mary Angelica and the baby, and hauled them off to a foundling home here in San Francisco.

"Sister Mary Angelica told me that the captain sent her into the home with the baby. He waited in the buggy outside. When she filled out the papers for the baby, she had to think of a name, but didn't dare put down her own, as Elizabeth wanted, because of the captain's wrath. She had become attached to Annabelle, as well as Elizabeth, so she decided to name her after them. As she thought over the names Annabelle Christine and Elizabeth Marie, she saw the relationship to her own name. Mary Angelica was similar to Marie Ann, but too similar, so she switched it to Anna Marie. Then she thought of the convent of St. James as the last name. The baby was called Anna Marie James.

"Sister Mary Angelica was the only one who knew this, other than Mother Superior at the convent, that is, until she passed the story on to me. For those few months she had been like a mother to the girls. I think they felt she had, in a sense, rescued them, by helping with the pregnancy, the baby, and teaching them so much. I believe that is why they left everything to Sister Mary Angelica.

"But, even beyond that, Sister Mary Angelica felt that they wanted the baby to have their inheritance. They didn't say that in the will, but they knew Sister was the only one who knew about the child, and cared about her. If they left their possessions to Sister Mary Angelica, then she could decide whether or not they should be passed on."

"Was there any further communication between the MacLean sisters and Sister Mary Angelica?" I asked.

"No. None."

"How about the baby? Did Sister Mary Angelica keep track of the baby?"

"Yes. She felt a certain attachment to the baby. So, later, she wrote to Sister Philippe at the foundling home and asked about it. Sister Philippe said a prominent family here had adopted the baby. She went to St. Mary's school here, and on to Magdalena College. Then she married a well-to-do young man. So you see why we haven't told this story before."

"Why now?" Bryan asked.

"Because Anna Marie has passed on. She had seven children, who are married and dispersed throughout the nation. And now, this new generation, is interested in looking for its roots. There is even a show on television about finding your roots. It seems a shame to deny anyone the truth, if it can help in some way. People aren't as snobbish as they were in the past. And I think that her great-grandchildren would appreciate having some of Elizabeth's things."

"Do you know where they live?"

"I believe part of the family is still here in San Francisco, but I'm not sure where. That's why I wanted to give you the information, and let you find them."

"We'd be happy to, Sister," I smiled.

"If you would like to do this, then once you have found them, you could have them contact me about Elizabeth's personal things. I'm sure the St. James convent wouldn't mind passing on some of the furniture and the portrait of Annabelle. They have more than enough furniture."

"Yes, we will, Sister. And thank you for all of the information and for your time. It has been very enjoyable."

"Yeah, thanks, Sister. We'll get right on it," said Bryan.

"Thank you both for being as interested in old houses as I am. Come, I'll show you Sister Mary Angelica's letter." Sister stood up, and we followed her inside.

As we walked back down the corridor toward the study, Sister told us that the MacLean house had become too expensive to keep up, so they had to sell it. She felt bad about it, because she loved the flower gardens there.

"Did you ever feel that the MacLean sisters were still present in that house?" I asked.

She looked surprised. "Why? Did you?"

"Yes, we…or…I felt like one of them wanted to tell me something. But I think that once the story is out, Elizabeth will rest peacefully." I was sticking my neck out, telling a nun that I believed in ghosts. Not sure what the Catholic belief on this was, I hoped she hadn't rescinded her faith in me.

"You too?" she said in a lowered voice. "I never told anyone this, but I did feel a presence, especially as I worked in the garden. I just knew that one of the MacLean sisters was there watching me."

"Didn't that scare you…living there?" I asked.

"No. I knew she was friendly and just concerned about her flowers. We had a mutual respect."

Bryan didn't say anything. I think he was surprised that a nun would make such an open confession. He couldn't believe in ghosts, even as open as he was to life.

I wrote down names and dates from Sister Ignatius' copy of Sister Mary Angelica's letter, while Bryan asked Sister Ignatius about some of the books in the room. We left, promising Sister Ignatius to let her know what we found out.

"So," said Bryan, as we headed down the hill, "do you want to investigate first? Or do you want to eat?"

"Bryan, we just ate a couple of hours ago. Are you hungry?"

"Well…yeah…sort of."

"I'm not hungry, and I'm dying to find out about Anna Marie's family. But, I'll tell you what."

"What?"

"Let's find a restaurant with a phone booth, where I can look up some names, and you can have a snack. Okay?"

"Okay. Here's one up ahead that looks old enough to have a phone booth."

As Bryan ate, I went over my notes. "First of all, Sister Mary Angelica kept up with Anna Marie from her adoption in 1900 by Mr. and Mrs. James Livingston, through her marriage to Matthew White in 1921 at age 21, and the births of her children Matthew 1923, Mark 1925, Luke 1928, John 1931, twins Mary and Martha 1936, and Anna, born in 1940, was named after her mother. And I have the spouses' names too.

"I'm starting with the youngest first, because of the way people die off or move away. Anna was born in 1940, so she must be about 65 now. She was married to Harold Burns in 1962 at age twenty-two. She could be divorced, or a widow, or remarried. That would be a problem. Okay, I'm going over to look through the phone book."

I looked in the San Francisco and Vicinity phone book and found Harold Burns there. I put the number into my cell phone and hit *send.*

A female voice answered. "Hello?"

"Hello? Mrs. Burns?" I asked.

"No. She isn't home right now. May I take a message?"

"Well, I'm not sure if I have the right Burns. Is her name Anna? And was her mother's name Anna Marie White?"

"Yes."

"Thank you, then I do have the right number. When do you expect her home?"

"She should be home by five."

"Okay. I'll call back then. Thank you so much."

"That's okay. Bye."

"Good bye." I closed my phone and sat back down with Bryan, smiling.

"Great! You got her!" Bryan smiled.

"Yes! Well, not her, but I think it was her daughter. She'll be home by five. That's not too long to wait. They live in San Raphael."

"Good. That's just over the Golden Gate Bridge. It's on our way back home. So, what do you want to do now?"

"I don't know. What do you suggest?"

"Would you like to see Golden Gate Park?"

"Oh, yes. I'd like that."

So, Bryan started in with the fifty-cent tour. "We don't have time to go into all of the buildings here, 'cause there's over a thousand acres. I'll just drive around and point out some of the things to you. There are a lot of gardens - the Botanical Garden, the Japanese Tea Garden, the Zen Garden, the Sculpture Garden, the Conservatory of Flowers, and the Dutch Tulip Garden with some old windmills."

"Wow, what a beautiful place!"

"Yeah. And see that old carousel over there with people on it? It's from the early 1900s, and was at the 1939 World Exposition on Treasure Island. And it's still going. Isn't that amazing?"

"It sure is. How do you know about all of this?"

"Well, I came here when I first moved to Milton. And I was so impressed at all there was to see, that I wrote an article for the Milton register about the park. There's even an aquarium and tide pools, a planetarium, an art museum, and buffalo."

"What? Did you say buffalo?"

"Yeah, well, they're really bison. They were brought here in the 1890s from Wyoming and Kansas. We'll drive by and see them."

We had been "driving by" everything I wanted to see. I wondered if we were ever going to stop. We didn't. He drove by the bison too… slowing a bit so I could see them. I was grateful for that. Then I asked, "Are we going to stop to see inside any of the buildings?"

"Yeah, sure. We're going to stop at Park Chalet."

I didn't know what the Park Chalet was, but I was thankful for small favors.

"The Park Chalet? What's that, an old ski lodge?"

"No, it's a restaurant and brewpub."

"I should have known!" I looked at him with a wary eye.

"Well, it's happy hour. We don't want to miss that. Do we?"

"I guess not." I was just happy to finally get out of his Jeep.

Chapter 10

Just Desserts or Karma

I was so anxious to talk to Anna Burns, I phoned at five on the dot. I told her who I was, and that I had been investigating the history of an old Victorian house up north, by the town of Milton. "And, I believe you are related to the family who first owned it. Would you like to hear about your mother's family?"

"You mean, the Livingston family?"

"No. The MacLean family."

"I don't know of any MacLean family. Are you sure you have the right Anna Burns?"

"Yes, I think I do. Was your mother Anna Marie James Livingston White?"

"Well, yes, she was Anna Marie Livingston White. But I don't know anything about James or MacLean."

"That's what I want to tell you. Your mother was adopted when she was a baby. Sister Mary Angelica named your mother when she was given to the foundling home here in San Francisco. And she kept up with your family through the newspapers. She wrote a letter telling all about your grandparents and great-grandparents. I've read the letter, and have been given permission to find you and tell you the story."

"Well, okay then. Can you come tonight at seven?"

"Yes. I am traveling with a friend, and we'll be there at seven."

Anna gave me her address, and we said goodbye.

"So, we meet them at seven, huh? Where do you want to have dinner?"

"You're the tour guide, Bryan. Lead the way."

We stayed where we were, at the Golden Gate Park Chalet Restaurant and Brewpub. We had a wonderful meal, and as we ate, we talked of the Victorian house in Milton, and of Elizabeth, Anna Marie, Sister Mary Angelica, and Sister Ignatius. And we wondered about Anna Burns. Would she believe what I had to tell her? And how would she take it?

"Do you think she might get mad at us for revealing that her mother was illegitimate?" I asked Bryan.

"I guess it depends on what socio-economical level she's in. We know that her father was well-to-do. Sister Mary Angelica wrote that. But, if she's working, she must not be rich."

"Unless she's working in a hospital or an institute as a volunteer. There are many well-to-do society women who do volunteer work, and put in almost as many hours as the employees. I know that for a fact, because my mother does that."

"Are you rich?" Bryan asked me.

"Not by a long shot! I haven't even received anything from the divorce. Why do you think I'm living in that shack on the beach?"

"Oh, I thought you liked slumming," he smiled at me. "But, you said your mom's a society lady, does a lot of volunteer stuff?"

"Yes, she does. My father is a surgeon at the hospital, so he is at the hospital a lot. So, she would stop by the hospital to see him, and she'd bring treats to the children there. And that escalated into holiday parties and fundraisers. They're well off, but not what you'd call rich."

"It doesn't matter whether you're rich or not, people are weird about what they want to hear about themselves."

"Yes, Bryan, but, on the other hand, I think that more people are open to new things now. Just look at the shows on TV. You see well-known movie stars writing books about their various affairs, admitting to having illegitimate babies by different fathers. And it's rare for them to get married these days. They just live together. It's easier. No commitments."

"I doubt that Anna Burns would ascribe to that."

I looked curiously at Bryan. "Why?" I asked.

"Because she's Catholic."

"Yes, but, because of this current, public, desensitization process, she might over-look a mistake in her own lineage."

"Could be," Bryan agreed.

"And she might be happy to know where her roots began... Scotland, I mean."

"Yeah, probably so. Anyway, all she can do is throw us out."

"Oh, Bryan, I don't think so. She sounded like a very nice person on the phone."

"I've talked to people on the phone, who turned into real barracudas in person."

"Maybe it's your electrifying magnetism that sets them off," I smiled.

"I don't know whether to take that as a compliment or an insult," he said seriously.

"I don't know either. I guess it's just a joke." I tried to weasel out of it, because I didn't want to be too serious with him. He had his own problems to solve. And it was difficult for me, wanting to advise him, yet not get involved. I thought, *Maybe, I could advise him in a subtle way.*

"Bryan, speaking of changing, if it hadn't been for that Victorian prudish attitude, Annabelle and Elizabeth wouldn't have locked themselves away in that house for the rest of their lives."

"I know. And, it's all the captain's fault. If he hadn't had such a temper, and restricted them to the house, they could have still gone to Europe and come out in society. No one would have known about the baby. When did he die, anyway?"

I looked through my notes. "1904, he was fifty-four. He was injured by a branch falling on his shoulder, and lost the use of his arm. Eventually, gangrene set in, and he refused to have it amputated. So he died…but they called it a heart attack."

"Just desserts for the selfish bastard," Bryan mused.

"My God, Bryan, that's it!"

"Huh? What?"

"I have a friend who is a retired English teacher, you know, Tom. I told you about him."

"The old guy that lives at the beach?"

"Yes. He has been telling me his theory about reincarnation. Have you read anything about it?"

"A little."

"Do you believe in it?"

"No…people coming back as animals? That belief hasn't done anything for the people starving on the streets in India."

"Don't forget, there are people starving on the streets in America too, who believe in Christianity. Besides, it's more than just that. People don't come back as animals. They come back in a higher form than when they left."

"You mean like little people from Mars with huge brains?"

"No. Tom says we reincarnate as babies, forgetting everything we knew before. Because, we wouldn't like ourselves if we remembered everything we did in a past life."

"We don't like ourselves now, in this life."

"Right. That's why we have to learn to forgive ourselves and others."

"That's easier said than done."

"I know. But back to reincarnation, the memory of past talents, interests, abilities and goals is locked up in our subconscious, to come out gradually, as we grow."

"Do you believe that?" he frowned.

"I don't know what I believe. I'm just listening and learning right now. I haven't come to the part where I have to accept or reject."

"So, what does this have to do with what I said about the captain being a selfish bastard?"

"According to Tom, we reap what we sow."

"According to Jesus, too."

"But, do we really reap what we sow? A man shoots another man. Does he get shot, too?"

"Sometimes."

"Yes, but not always."

"Well, you don't have to take it literally, Laura. It means that whatever rotten things you do here on earth, you'll have to pay for it in purgatory."

"I'm not ruling that out, Bryan. But, what if…and it is possible… what if we got it back, here on earth, either in this life or the next life?"

"So, you're saying, that when we get to purgatory, God says, *Look at what you did. Now, go back down there and get punished for it.* It doesn't make sense. He might as well punish us for it now, while we're here. It'd save us both a lot of trouble."

"I said practically the same thing to Tom. And he said we need to review how we've acted, and change our attitude, and repent, and to develop spiritually, and want to try again. It's not the hand of God that comes down on us, so to speak. It's our own guilty feelings that make us want to atone. I can believe this, because guilt is one of the greatest causes of psychosis. It makes me wonder if some of the guilt that I see in my patients hasn't come from a past life."

"I don't know, Laura. I don't know about psychology or about other religions, but I do know that the priests in our church, throughout the world and through the centuries have studied theology and psychology extensively. And if they haven't discovered it for themselves, then I'm not going to believe what an old guy on the beach says."

"That's okay. I'm not saying you have to believe it. I'm not saying I believe it. I'm just investigating the subject, and trying to see if it works. That's where your statement comes in. I suddenly realized, that it was very symbolic of his life."

"Whose life?"

"The captain's. He was selfish and tyrannical to his daughters. He wouldn't allow them out of the house, or anyone in. He punished them by making them work in the house. He was not open or understanding toward them. Consequently, he lost the use of his arm, his hand and his life."

"Oh, come on, Laura. That's a little far-fetched."

"No. It's all very symbolic. He would not reach out his arms to his daughters. He pushed them away. So he lost the use of his arm. He took away their chance to live, to have a normal, happy life. So, he lost his life. An eye for an eye, and a life for a life."

"Look, Laura, I know guys that have spent their lives making it hell for others, and they are perfectly happy, and even successful."

"Wait a minute, Bryan. You really can't say that they are happy, because no one knows the mind of another. And, who's to say what success is? It's a very relative word. There have been college graduates, who have had honors throughout school, gone into a good paying job, have had wife and family, beautiful home, and were what everyone looked up to as happy and successful. Then suddenly, this supposedly "happy" person would commit suicide and no one would know why."

"Yeah, I've heard of cases like that, too. I guess you can't say who is successful, if you look at it that way. But you must admit, everyone doesn't get paid off for what they do to others."

"Maybe not in this lifetime. But, maybe in the next. Why are babies born blind, crippled or deformed?"

"Accident at birth, disease or genetics."

"That's what we call it. But, some people call it karma."

"My God, Laura, that's as bad as believing in witchcraft! Why can't people just accept what the Bible says?"

"Because it's so contradictory. That's why we have so many religions in this world. Besides, it's been changed over the years."

"Not *our* Bible."

"Whose Bible?"

"The Catholic Bible."

I didn't argue the point with him, that Constantine and the Council of Nicea changed the wording of the Bible, and even threw out several chapters that they didn't agree with. After all…I had to ride back home with him. So, I went about it in a different way.

"Let's just suppose there was something to this idea. If there is a perfect law and order to the universe, then there must be a reason for everything. We don't know all of the reasons, but we have subconscious feelings about things. Your mind can make you do things you wouldn't ordinarily do. Like a mother's fear for her child could make her shoot a stranger at her door."

"Yeah?"

"And, it's known that past experiences can make us react in a certain way in a particular situation. The mind does funny things. It can make us suddenly believe something we weren't aware of before. Like a girl says to her friend, *Hey, that guy really likes you.* It may not be true, but the friend starts noticing this guy, she may not have bothered with before. Pretty soon, she has a full-blown infatuation, without the guy doing a thing. She developed this romance in her head. Not unlike the wet dreams you men have in your sleep." I grinned at him.

"Come on now, let's not get personal," Bryan defended himself.

"Sorry. Just giving you another example of how the mind can hallucinate to the point of functional embarrassment."

"Okay. You win. But, you still haven't convinced me about the old guy dying because of the way he treated his daughters."

"I'm not saying it is so, either, Bryan. Just that, it's a possibility... something to think about."

"Well, I'm not going to waste my time thinking about it."

I could see that he wasn't interested in the subject, so I changed it. "Regardless of a karmic connection, there is a natural law of cause and effect which governs our lives."

"Like what?"

"Well, the way we treat others is the way we get treated back."

"Not always."

"Okay, give me an example of when it doesn't work." I was completely open to any new ideas he could offer me, since this was still an incubation period in my psychic awareness.

"I treated my wife and my best friend good. Look how they repaid me."

I didn't dare say that maybe there was some connection among the three of them from a past life. Maybe he really was getting paid back for doing the same thing to them in another life. I didn't know enough about it to even discuss it with him. So, I just let it go.

"Okay, Bryan. There are things that we don't understand, but basically, if you treat someone kindly, they'll be kind to you. Don't you agree?"

"I suppose. If the person is normal."

"Right. It depends on the person's level of consciousness how he treats you. There are people like sociopaths and psychopaths who can't be trusted under any circumstances. But, let's talk about basically normal people."

"Like me?" he grinned.

"Yes. Like you." I smiled back.

"You are carrying around hate for two people. And that hate might result in your losing your child."

"Why do you say that?" He frowned at me.

"Well, you told me that you will contact Debby when she graduates from high school. That's a long time. You're assuming she'll want to see you then. She might not. She might feel that you've rejected her all of these years. So, why should she bother with you now?"

"'Cause I'm her dad."

"She won't remember you as her dad. Her only dad will be your ex-friend, because he fed her, clothed her, took her to school and was there when she was sick."

"Well, I can't do anything about that."

"Yes, you can. You can start communicating with her now. She doesn't know that you love her, unless you tell her so. Don't wait until she's eighteen."

"Carol might not even let her have my letters. She hates me."

"How do you know?"

"At the custody hearing, she said rotten things about me, so she could get Debby."

"That was a long time ago, Bryan. Her attitude may have changed toward you. Guilt plays a big part in changing attitudes."

"Yeah, maybe you're right. Maybe she does feel a little guilty."

"Then, if she does, she should be willing to talk to you."

"Maybe."

"It doesn't hurt to try. The best way to keep in touch with your daughter is to keep in communication with her mother."

"Yeah, maybe you're right. But I'm not going to call. Pete might answer. I don't want to talk to him. I'll write a letter to her." Bryan was thoughtful, seemingly thinking about it...possibly composing the letter in his head.

"I'll tell her I'd like to write to Debby and maybe see her a few times during the year. Hell, all she can say is no. Actually, she can't say that, either, 'cause I have visiting rights. She can give me some static, but in the long run, I'll win. Good! I'll do it!"

"You see how fast you can change your attitude? Do you feel better now?"

"Yeah. I do. I think it will work."

"It will, because your change of attitude will have to result in a different feeling on her part. The next goal will be to forgive your friend."

"Oh, that'll be a cold day in hell!"

"Falling in love usually can't be helped. We need to see the weaknesses in others, and recognize that we have those same weaknesses."

"The hell we do! I'd never go after my best friend's wife!"

"Bryan, you don't know what you would do, until you are actually doing it. These things aren't premeditated."

"With him it was!"

"How do you know?"

"'Cause they were sneaking around behind my back."

"Where were you at the time?"

"On assignments. And he'd come by the house when he knew I was out of town."

I could see that Bryan was getting riled up again, and I didn't want him to think I was against him by trying to defend Pete and Carol. So, I changed the subject.

"It's close to seven. I guess we'd better get going. The Burns family will be waiting for us. I just hope they are open to all of this."

"Yeah. It's a big mystery, isn't it?"

"Yes, it sure is. It has been a mystery to me all the way...the story of the house, the captain, Katherine, Annabelle, Elizabeth, the servants, the nuns, and now Anna Marie's family."

The Burns house was an average income tract home. It was a one-storied, white, ranch-style house, suitable for a family of four. We rang the bell.

"Hi!" A lady of medium height, short brown hair and a cheerful smile greeted us.

"Hi! I'm Laura, and this is my friend Bryan."

"It's good to meet you. I'm Anna. Please come in."

She introduced her husband, Harold, who was red-haired, medium height, stocky and jovial. We sat in the living room, as I told the story about the house and the MacLean family. Anna was very open to hearing about her mother's heritage. She listened intently as Bryan and I described the house and explained our interest in it. I even told about the meeting with Mrs. Erickson, coming up that week, and asked if they would like to join our psychic exploration of the house on Thursday.

"Nope," said Harold. "I can't take the time off work."

"Well, I'm interested," said Anna. "But, I don't have any more time off, either. Maybe we could come up on a weekend, and bring our daughter, Amy. She works at the Pizza Palace, but maybe she can get the time off. She graduated from Berkeley with a degree in horticulture, but couldn't find work in that field, so she's working at the Pizza Palace temporarily." Anna sounded hopeful.

"Oh, Amy likes to work with flowers?" I asked.

"Yes, Amy has always loved working with flowers and plants. As a child, she would gather seeds from plants outside, and put them into pots, and tend them until they grew into maturity. She has always made gifts of plants, pottery and decorated baskets with various crafts she made from dried flowers."

"Well, she gets that from her great-grandmother, Elizabeth. She loved to work in her garden, too."

"Come, I'll show you Amy's garden."

We walked through the house, as Anna pointed out various things that Amy had made. Then she put on the porch light so we could see the backyard. It was neatly organized into areas of profuse flowers and foliage.

"This is beautiful," I said. "The gardens at the MacLean house must have looked like this at one time."

"Yes. It's so sad to see a garden that has been neglected, after all of the work someone has put into it. Amy wanted to get a job at a nursery, but the pizza job came up first, and she needed the job to help pay her college loan. So, eventually she'll find a job working with plants."

"I'm sure she will. It's obvious that she has a great love for it."

Bryan and I left the Burns home feeling good about our visit. We knew we would hear from Anna sometime soon.

Chapter 11

The Gazebo

The day after our trip to San Francisco, I drove into Milton to get a few groceries. On my return to the beach, I decided to drive by the old Victorian house on the cliff. I was compelled, as if a voice was saying, *Go by and see if it's still there,* sort of a hitting home-base feeling. It was as if I needed to have the house refreshed in my memory, so I could continue connecting the story with something tangible.

David's van was there. So I stopped. I followed the walkway around the side of the house. On the cliff side of the house, I saw David sitting on a short stool in front of his easel, concentrating on the gazebo.

"Hi, David!" I called out before I reached the gazebo, so I wouldn't startle him by coming too close. I know that sudden shock to the system, when you're deep in concentration, and someone comes upon you and says something. It's like they're shouting at you. It takes a while to settle back down. I learned not to do this when visiting my grandmother in San Clemente. She would be so intent when cooking, crocheting or gardening, sometimes when I spoke to her, it startled her. And I felt so bad for doing that. And I felt bad for her, too.

David had quite a bit of the gazebo painted. "Hi, Laura. How are you doing?"

"Oh, fine. I just went into town to get a few things, and thought I'd come by and see if the old place was still standing."

"Yep. It's still here. This is one of the prettiest gazebos I've seen. I've been coming the last few days to get the morning sun on it."

"It *is* pretty, in spite of the paint peeling off. Wouldn't it be beautiful painted white, with flowers growing all around it?"

"Yeah. And, a beautiful girl sitting inside of it. I can just picture her. Laura, sit in there and let me see how you look."

"In jeans and sweatshirt? I doubt that I'd make a very pretty picture."

"You underestimate the extent of my imagination."

"Sorry, David. You're right. Okay, I'll pose for you. But promise me you'll do something different with my hair."

"Don't worry. It's just the basic outline that I need."

"Good. You can slim that down a bit, too, while you're at it."

"Oh, you women are all alike, never satisfied."

"That's life! If a person were perfectly satisfied with herself, she wouldn't need to keep on striving for perfection. Then there would be no need to keep on living."

"God! Are *you* the philosopher this morning!" David positioned me on the bench inside of the gazebo, tilting my head down. I gave the intruding weeds on the rotting floor a pensive look.

"Good!" said David. "Hold that look! Don't move!"

"Can I talk?" I sat like a stone nymph sitting by a pond, staring into the water.

"Sure. Tell me what's making you so gloomy this morning?"

"Well, besides the floor looking like it's going to rot out from under me, I found out the sad story of this house." As I said this, a cold chill went through me. Then, as suddenly as it came, it left. And I felt a ray of sunlight on my cheek, as it stole through the latticed roof.

"Good! Tell me about it. Just don't move!"

"Okay. Well, you know about the two MacLean sisters. One had a coming-out party and the other didn't. What happened was, their father, the captain, had commissioned a young artist to paint the girls for their sixteenth birthdays, as a present to them. The young artist was from San Francisco, but the captain put him up in a hotel in Milton. He painted Annabelle in the springtime, so her picture was finished for her party in June. Then he painted Elizabeth's portrait in the summertime.

I guess the captain figured he'd get them both done while he had the young artist here. The pictures were to hang over the two fireplaces in the ballroom for Elizabeth's coming out party the following year."

"Sure. He wanted them to look alike. You get a different artist, and they might not match in colors and conformation. In those days, he might not be able to find the same guy a year later."

"Yes. So, the young artist painted Elizabeth's portrait, and she fell in love with him."

"Uh oh! Trouble."

"That's right. She got pregnant. Wouldn't tell anyone about it until the picture was done. And the artist was taking a long time painting, so he could be with her. So, he must have loved her too."

"Or else, he didn't want his meal ticket to end."

"Just how do you mean that, David?"

"Room and board. He didn't want that to end."

"Okay, that's possible. But, I like to think that he really did love her." I looked up at David.

"Hey, keep your head still. So, what happened then?"

"When the captain came home from his trip, Elizabeth told him, hoping he would let them marry. The captain stormed out of the house, and that night both the artist and the two portraits disappeared."

"He destroyed them?"

"No, because the picture of Annabelle hangs at the convent."

"What about the other picture?"

"No one knows. He must have destroyed Elizabeth's portrait. Then, Annabelle hid her picture so he wouldn't destroy it. She must have brought it out after the captain died."

"What happened to the baby?"

"Sister Mary Angelica, a young nurse from the convent, came to live with them and help with the pregnancy and delivery. Then the captain drove Sister Mary Angelica and the baby to an orphanage in San Francisco. The nun named the baby after the combined names of Annabelle and Elizabeth Marie…Anna Marie. Anna Marie was adopted, as a baby, by a prominent family in San Francisco. She married and had seven kids."

"Wow! That's recompense for being an only child!"

"And a good Catholic."

"I guess! What then?"

"As you know, the MacLean sisters lived a life of solitude."

"Imprisonment is more like it."

"In those days, people lived with a lot of guilt. They would rather imprison themselves than face shame."

"So, no one ever found out? What about the servants?"

"They were fired and sent away immediately. They didn't know about the pregnancy, but were fired for allowing the romance in the captain's absence. Sister Mary Angelica and the Mother Superior at that time were the only ones who knew about it. The sister was like a mother to them. They loved her. That's part of why they left everything to her."

"What's the other part?"

"Well, nuns can't own anything. And anything given to them belongs to the church. But, in the will, Annabelle and Elizabeth said that the house, furniture and all of their possessions should go to Sister Mary Angelica, to be held until someone came for them."

"And did they?"

"No. No one ever found out about Anna Marie's background, because her adoptive parents never told her that she was adopted."

"How did you find out about all of that?"

"Bryan and I went to San Francisco yesterday and talked with Sister Ignatius. She is the nun who was given the information by Sister Mary Angelica. She said it was time the story was told. She realized that people are searching for their roots now, and she didn't want to deny that opportunity to this family."

"Even if it is a prominent family?"

"Yes. She gave us permission to find Anna Marie's family. I think she trusted us to be discreet, because Bryan is Catholic, and I'm a psychoanalyst."

"You can't always count on that!"

"I know, David. But, I think Sister Ignatius has had many years of experience in reading people."

"So, did you find them?"

"Yes. We did. Anna Marie's youngest child, Anna, married Harold Burns, and they live in San Rafael. They have two children, a son, Michael, who's married and has two children, and a daughter, Amy, who just graduated from Berkeley."

"How did they take the news that grandma was illegitimate?"

"Well, we only saw Anna and Harold. She seemed to be okay with it. She was happy to hear the whole story."

"No doubt...that Bohemian artist grandfather's blood in her."

"Possibly. I think she was a bit of a renegade, because she married a non-Catholic."

"Oh, and was disinherited, no doubt."

"Possibly, but more likely there wasn't much left, after dividing it among seven kids. Both she and her husband work. And, they live in an average income residence. They're not rich, but comfortable."

"Is she going to come up here and see the house?"

"They both said they'd like to, but can't come until the weekend, because they work. I told them about Mrs. Erickson, and you getting us together on Thursday. But they said they couldn't come."

"How did they react to the psychic thing?"

"Well, they didn't throw us out. I guess they were tolerant of the idea. They were interested in seeing the house and the things at the convent. They were really nice. I hope they do come up here."

"Yeah. That'd be cool. Okay, you can relax now. I have you all formed in."

"Good. I was beginning to get a kink in my neck. I don't know how models sit still for so long."

"Talking helps. It gets your mind off your body. Like in the dentist's chair, they have music piped in to soothe your nerves. And the dentist talks to you all the time he's drilling on your teeth."

"I know. All I can do is think of things I want to answer back, but can't. It's frustrating, but it *does* keep your mind off the drilling… somewhat. I hate the sound of the drill!"

"Me too. But I discovered that the seagulls at the beach have the same sound as the drill. So when I'm under the drill, I visualize being at the beach and watching the seagulls."

"What a good idea! I'll have to try it! Can I get up now?"

"Sure. Come and look. I don't have the face in, but the hair and dress are starting to look like something."

"Oh, David! It's going to be beautiful! I'm glad you put an old-fashioned dress on her. But why brunette? You don't like my blonde hair?"

"No, it's not that. It's that I've been thinking about this girl for a long time. She's been on my mind ever since I dreamed about her. She is small, delicate and sweet."

"Every man's dream!" I chided him.

"No. I see her very clearly. When I painted the girl in the window, it was just a shadow of her…just a form, no face. But, I had a dream the other night that I was here at this house, standing outside painting the gazebo. I guess I dreamed that because I've been thinking of doing it.

"But, anyway, sitting in the gazebo was a girl, dark haired, wearing a light, flowing dress. Her head was tilted down, and she had sort of a sweet look. When she looked up at me, her eyes were dark and round, with long dark eyelashes, and I felt a glow of love pour through me. It was so wonderful. I woke up still feeling that love. I guess you would say this is the girl of my dreams."

"I guess so, David. You are lucky you're able to paint her. There is a certain sense of fulfillment to a dream, when you're able to reproduce it into something tangible."

"I don't know if I can do her the justice she deserves, but I'll try my darnedest."

"Then I suppose you'll spend the rest of your life searching for that girl?"

"Maybe. Or someone like her. Do you suppose that dream was a prophecy?"

"It could be, David. It's been known to happen. On the other hand, Tom might say that it's reliving a past life."

"Really? I didn't know he believed in reincarnation. I'll have to talk to him about that. Something I've always wondered about is déjà vu. How do they explain that, anyway?"

"I don't know how Tom would explain it, but psychiatrists define it as a short glitch in electrical connections in the brain. And, psychologists think of it as a short trip into clairvoyance. The idea that you have experienced something before, or that you know what someone is going to say before they say it, is thought to be a quick flash of precognition. It's very common…a trick of the mind."

"It's really weird. You really think you're reliving an experience."

"Tom would probably say you are. But, no one really knows."

"I don't know. From what I've read about reincarnation, each time you come back, your life is different and better."

"How can it be better, David, if you are atoning for past transgressions?"

"It may not seem better, if you're crippled or in a situation that's full of conflict. But it's a step up the ladder of awareness. We might think we're suffering, but it's really a learning experience. And we come out a better person from it."

"Well, David, some learning experiences don't make you a better person. In fact, in cases of abuse, there is a lot of mental destruction, which often breeds further abuse. How do you explain that?"

"Yeah, I know. I've read about how a person who beats his kids was beaten by his parents. Somehow, they think it's the way you're supposed to do."

"They confuse it with love, David. Because that's the only attention they got from their parents. And so it goes, until someone finally gets professional help."

"Yeah, it's not only the beating on, but it's the thinking behind it that causes the problem."

"I know. That's a psychological fact. But how can you say this is a better life, a learning experience for the person being abused?"

"Maybe the kid being beaten on, had beaten his wife and kids in another life. Now he gets it back."

"But it doesn't help him if he goes on doing it to his family, when he gets married. It just breeds more abusers."

"The way I see it is, if I was an abuser in a past life, now in this life when I'm beaten, I hate it and abhor any kind of violence, and become a peaceful man. But, when we have been violent and abusive in many past lives, it takes many life experiences for us to grow out of that attitude. But with each life we get better, until we have learned the lesson. That's why not all of the abused become abusers."

"Well, that's an interesting way of thinking of it. I'll have to give it some thought."

"I have a good book for you to read, Laura. It's called, *Many Mansions* by Gina Cerminara. I'll bring it tomorrow."

"Thanks. I'd like that."

Chapter 12

Amy Arrives

Anna and Harold didn't come. But Amy did.

"Hello, Dr. Christopher?"

"Yes?" I wondered what young lady in Milton would know my name and number.

"I'm Amy Burns, Anna Marie White's granddaughter. My mom told me about your visit to our house this week, and I just had to come."

"Yes, Amy. I'm so glad to hear that. Where are you now?"

"I'm in Milton. I left this afternoon, and just got here. I wanted to see the house."

"Great! I live at the beach. You take highway 1 and drive about two miles south from Milton, and you'll see a sign that says *Beach Road.* Turn right there and follow it to Sea View Road. Turn left onto Sea View Road. The house number is 79. If you get lost, just call me."

"Okay, I'll be right there."

"Good. See you soon."

I was happy that Amy had come. It gave me a more concrete connection to the house. I could tell from her voice, that we'd have a good time together.

From the moment I opened the door, she started talking about all of the things her mother had said about me and the house and her grandmother and great-grandmother.

"I'm so glad you could come, Amy. Can you stay for a few days?"

"Yes. I brought a suitcase. I was hoping you had room for me."

"I have a couch, if you don't mind sleeping on it."

"That's fine. I was ready to sleep on the floor, if I had to."

I served coffee and some store-bought cookies, and we talked. Amy was a lovely girl. She had long, curly brown hair, which tapered around her face and ended at her shoulders. Her dark brown eyes seemed to be eagerly searching for the truth. Their wide, round honesty compelled one's attention to them. A multi-layered outfit neglected to hide her petite figure. Dimpled cheeks and chin gave an elfin quality to her exuberance.

As we chattered away, my phone rang. It was David.

"Hi, Laura. I just wanted you to know it's all set for tomorrow. I called Mrs. Erickson and Sam Griffin, and they'll meet us at the house at noon."

"And Bryan wants to come too," I added.

"I don't have his number. Do you wanna call him and tell him the time?"

"Yes, I will. And I have a surprise for you, David."

"Really? What?"

"Elizabeth MacLean's great-granddaughter is here at my place. She wants to see the house, too."

"Great! Is she good looking?"

"Yes, a doll. Why don't you come over and meet her?"

"I will. By golly! I will."

"Nothing more curious than an artist," I said to Amy, as I closed my phone.

"Unless it's a bucket of amateur sleuths," Amy added.

"Right!" I laughed. "That's what we are, all right. David teaches art at the high school. He's single and really cute! He's on his way over, anxious to meet you."

"Good. I want to meet him too, with *that* recommendation."

"And Bryan is the newspaper guy I came to San Francisco with. Your parents met him."

"Yeah, they told me."

"I have to give him a call. Maybe he'd like to come over, too. He should be off work about now."

I called Bryan, told him about David's call and about Amy being there, and he said he'd be right over. Amy and I straightened our hair and faces a bit. Then, Amy sat on the deck looking out at the ocean, while I made a fresh pot of coffee, and put a frozen casserole into the oven.

The men must have been thinking along the same lines, because Bryan arrived with a six-pack of beer, pop, and two pizzas. And David brought a bottle of white wine and a bucket of chicken.

"Wow! What a feast," Bryan exclaimed. "We can eat all night!"

"That's what you think!" I glanced warily at him, with a hint of humor.

Through lively conversation, we devoured pizza, chicken, and noodle casserole. David and Amy immediately began talking about college. He had gone to Berkeley, as well. They reminisced about classes, professors and dorm activity. Meanwhile, Bryan confided to me that he had written a letter to his ex-wife, Carol.

"But, then I read it over, and it sounded like I was apologizing, and I didn't want that. So, finally, after planning out the whole dialogue in my mind, I decided to phone. I was ready for whoever answered. But Carol answered, and we had a good conversation. I was surprised that it was so easy to talk to her. She was friendly and happy to hear from me. She said she would bring Debby out for a visit in a couple of weeks."

Bryan's spirits were soaring. He was like a different person. We chatted away as animatedly as Amy and David. More as an observer this evening, I watched David's boyish charisma enchant and enrapture Amy. And I noted, with curiosity, Bryans change in attitude. Was it in anticipation of seeing his daughter, Debby? Or Carol? Or just the relief of letting go of his burden of hate? Maybe it was all three.

After dinner, Bryan made a fire in the fireplace. Bryan and I sat on the couch, while David and Amy sat on the floor close to the fire. I was so pleased at how well David and Amy were getting along. Bryan, whose stomach was always thinking of food, made some popcorn. We ate popcorn and drank beer and wine, and talked late into the night. It was a wonderful evening, and I was so happy for David's and Amy's friendship, that when Bryan leaned over and kissed me, I let him.

David kissed Amy, too. I was surprised. It was a long, meaningful kiss; as if this weren't the first time they had met. I was almost envious of them. Their kiss looked a whole lot better than the one I had just been given.

After they left, Amy and I talked about them.

"He's wonderful! He's gorgeous! He's so neat!"

"Is this love at first sight?" I smiled.

"I think so. I didn't want him to go. I wanted to go home with him. And I'm not that kind of girl!"

"Are you sure it's not just infatuation? He is really cute. I'd say he'd make most any young girl fall for him. I would, if I were his age."

"Laura, it's as if we've known each other all our lives. I've never felt like this about anyone else…ever. I feel so comfortable with him. I didn't want him to leave."

"I'm happy for you, Amy. He really is a nice person…talented and sincere."

"Yes, he is. Bryan seems to be very nice too." Amy looked at me questioningly.

"He is nice. But, there's nothing serious about our relationship…yet, anyway."

"Well, it looked like there was something brewing between you two tonight."

"That was actually the first time he has kissed me. He's nice, and fun to date, but he's a little too rigid in his thinking for me. I like a guy that is flexible, open to new ideas and ways of thinking. I don't think I could marry someone who sees everything as purely black or white."

"Gee, you'd think he'd be more open, being a reporter."

"I know, Amy. But being a reporter doesn't necessarily mean a person is giving both sides of the story. Lots of reporters add their own opinion to the news. In fact, maybe that's what makes them go into newspaper work, because they like to tell their opinion of things."

"Maybe so. What is it that he is so opinionated about?"

"Don't get me wrong. He isn't stubborn or argumentative. But, when a person says, *I don't want to talk about that,* or hear about it, then I question their openness. And as husband and wife, that can be a big problem. People need to be able to talk about anything and everything before they consider marriage. Because, it doesn't get any better afterward."

"Yeah, I can imagine. Did you hear David and me? It seems like we could talk all night long without ever stopping."

"Yes. I noticed. It was as if you were trying to put a lifetime into one evening."

"I felt as though we did. I can't wait till tomorrow, to see the house and see David again."

"Then, lets go to bed, so it will come sooner."

"Good idea."

I made a bed on the couch for Amy, and told her, "If you wake up before me, help yourself to whatever you want in the kitchen. I like to sleep in. But check the beach for David. He likes to paint early in the morning. You never know where he'll pop up."

"Okay, I will. And thanks for everything. I'm so glad I came."

"I'm glad too, Amy. It sort of completes the whole story."

That night, I dreamed a series of dreams that were fast-paced and intense. When I awakened, I jotted down the main ideas before I forgot them:

Dream 1- cars, campers, roadblock, policeman lookout, Ronald Reagan speaking, don't remember words. Dream 2- Bryan & I climbing Mt., steep, precarious, he's confident, I'm unsure, hi ledge, animals sitting across ledge. He climbs toward animals. I don't want to go, but I hand him some tools to hang onto, like hooks. There's a board he stands on to balance h/s to get from one ledge to other where animals are. Dream 3- Bryan & I on small island surrounded by water, standing outside of Victorian house. Wonder how we'll get off island. It moves. Island floating on water. It's stable, but feels insecure. I like house, but don't want it here. Wish I could move it to another place. Dream 4- I suddenly realize I don't have my purse, left it in my car. Remember car is unlocked. I go to car. I see some men in black leaving, & think they stole my purse. I look in window of car & see purse is there & all is ok. I wonder why robbers didn't take my purse. Decide nothing they wanted. Think I shouldn't carry so much stuff in my purse. Wake up.

When I finished writing down my dreams, I listened to see if Amy was up. I couldn't hear her, so I stayed in bed and wrote about my dreams.

I could see that all of these dreams were saying basically the same thing. They were answering the questions that were on my mind as I went to sleep. Should I become involved with Bryan? Is he sincere? Does he still love his wife? Would I be left out in the cold? Is it better not to become too attached? What should I be doing?

The first dream is telling me to stop and think. *I'm traveling in the car. The roadblock stops me.* The car indicates the way I'm going. *I'm in the driver's seat.* I'm in control of my life. Campers symbolize mobility in home life. Right now my life is like living in a camper. I'm in between any permanency, sort of on the move. *The policeman stops me.* This is my higher authority saying, *Wait, stop and take a look! He seems to be looking out for something. Then President Reagan is making a speech.* This means there is something important here that I must be aware of. *Stop, Look, and Listen!* What am I to stop, look and listen to?

Dream 2 tells me the answer. *It has me climbing a mountain with Bryan.* This shows progress, growth, and upward mobility. What are our feelings? *Bryan is confident, even though the way is steep and precarious. I'm unsure, and afraid of falling...falling from where he is leading me. The high ledge is a plateau,* in a sense, a level of attainment. What is he trying to attain?

The animals are not vicious, and they aren't tame. They are just wild forest animals. The wildness symbolizes our animal instincts. Bryan is striving, through his animal instincts. I'm afraid to go with mine. Maybe this dream is saying I should.

On the other hand, animal instincts also have a sexual connotation. Bryan is striving toward sexual satisfaction, and I'm holding back. This is the conflict within me. What should I do?

I hand Bryan some hooks to hang onto. Just like I did when I gave him some ideas about getting in touch with his daughter, Debby, and ex-wife, Carol. Those hooks I gave him helped him to achieve greater success.

This is shown in the dream by *him reaching the board and standing on it, to cross the ledge where the animals are. He is balancing.* Maybe he is balancing his feelings about Carol and me. Or maybe the board is symbolic of my needing to balance the animal instincts with the fears that are holding me back. The question is, which is reality? The basic animal drives, or thoughtful cognizance? Maybe the next dream tells me.

Dream 3 *has Bryan and me on an island. We are isolated, and surrounded by water. I'm wondering how we'll get off the island. I feel the island floating. I feel that it is stable, but insecure.* This is me I'm talking about...about how I'm feeling. Yet, Bryan and I on an island, shows that the dream is isolating us. It shows that this dream is about our relationship.

The old Victorian house is a symbol of me living in the past. *We are walking around outside of it.* This is what's going on outside of me. The old Victorian house symbolizes my old-fashioned ideas. This dream is trying to straighten me out from the misconception about the animal instincts of the second dream. I didn't get it then, so now I'm seeing it a different way.

Okay, *the island is floating – it is stable, but insecure.* That's our relationship, a good, strong friendship, but not secure enough to become tied down and permanent. Then, the Victorian house is symbolic of sticking with the old fashioned ideas of morality. *I like it, but want to move on.* This dream is saying I should look around and not stay in one place, or with one person right now.

Now, the last dream is saying, *Don't worry. Things will take care of themselves!* Not having my purse shows insecurity, just like the mountain and the island. These are the feelings of insecurity and instability that keep coming over me, in my dreams, and during the day.

Then I realize my purse is in my car. I feel momentarily relieved, until I realize my car is unlocked…insecurity again. I go to my car, and see robbers leaving it. Again, I have heightened fears. The dark figures are the fears, doubts and worries that plague me about my future. This dream is showing me how these insecure feelings keep coming up in me, and rob me of a sense of self-confidence.

I look through the car window. Looking through a window is seeing things more clearly. This says to open my eyes and see that everything is okay. *I see my purse is there,* and now I feel secure.

I wonder why the robbers didn't take my purse. Then I decide there was nothing they wanted in there. This is telling me not to worry about what will happen, to just be open and aware, and everything will be okay.

At the end of the dream I think I shouldn't carry so much stuff in my purse. This shows that I have learned the lesson of the dream; I have decided to get rid of the baggage I've been carrying around…the doubts and fears. And I wake up.

I don't always remember so many dreams in one night. Sometimes I only remember a fragment of a dream, or just one dream. But, dream lab studies show that we dream four or five dreams a night.

We just don't remember dreaming. However, the lesson comes out during the day in flashes of insight.

Usually the dreams in one night are about the same subject. Your mind gives you the story in different ways, so you can see it from different angles and learn the lesson.

I have found, the dream shows its purpose at the beginning. Then in the middle, it shows me what is going on in my life and how I'm reacting. Then at the end it shows the solution.

Each of these dreams had the same problem in mind...the problem that I went to bed thinking about. The first dream said, "*Laura, stop, look and listen to what's happening with you!*" The second dream said, "*This is the way things are going with you and Bryan. He's striving, using his animal instincts, and you aren't. You're unsure of yourself and holding back.*"

Then the third dream said, "*Now, this is what you should do. Realize that the foundation of this relationship is insecure. Follow your Victorian values. Look around.*"

The thought of looking around brought on worries and insecurities again, like the fear of losing my purse, with all of it's valuables. But, the robbers showed that what I thought was valuable, really wasn't. Therefore, there is no need to worry. It really is relative to your own thinking.

Everything is relative. If I lost a purse with just two dollars in it, and no credit cards or cell phone, I wouldn't worry about it, unless it was my only purse, and my only two dollars. If I lost my purse with $50, phone and credit cards in it, I'd be upset, unless I immediately called and cancelled my phone and credit cards. So, worry is strictly relative to the individual's thinking. And that can be changed.

Chapter 13

A Mystical Discovery

After analyzing my dream, I got dressed, made a pot of coffee and sat on the deck eating an orange. Amy was still asleep on the couch. It was about 10 o'clock when Amy appeared in the doorway. There was no doubt what she had in mind. She was wearing a bikini. What a petite figure she had! It was slim, but very shapely. Her hair was pulled back into a ponytail and she was barefooted.

"Hi! I'm going to see if David is out here. Then, I'm going to lie in the sun." She headed down the steps to the beach.

"Don't you want something to eat? Egg? Cereal? Coffee?" I yelled after her.

"No thanks. I never eat before noon."

Now I knew the secret of that tiny waist.

"Okay, I'll watch the time so you don't get burned."

"I'm okay. I slathered my body with sunscreen."

"Good. Then I won't worry about you."

I went inside and got myself a cup of coffee, and stepped back out onto the deck. It was a quiet morning at the beach…only the gulls and pipers swooping and running on the sand. As the tide receded, the birds followed it to its ebb, picking up mini-morsels along their way. The sun was warm, and the sea breeze cool and quieting.

I walked out on the beach and looked toward the cliff, where the Victorian house stood. Then I realized that Amy didn't know where it was. She was slowly walking along the beach, so I caught up to her.

"Come on, Amy, I'll show you the house."

"Oh, can we see it from here?"

"Yes, somewhat. You see that old dock down there?"

"Uh-huh."

"That used to be a long dock where ships came in and delivered goods to these big homes along here. Your great-great-grandfather, Captain MacLean, had it built. If you look directly from the dock to the cliff, you will see some broken down stairs. They went up to the MacLean house. You have to get over here closer to the water to see the house."

"Oh, yes! And there's David. Hi David! David!"

"He can't hear you, because of the ocean. He's still painting the gazebo."

"Oh, Laura," she exclaimed excitedly, "can we go up there now?"

"Sure, I guess so. We have to drive up there. But, we should change our clothes first, because we'll be meeting Sam, the realtor, and Mrs. Erickson, the psychic, at noon. Are you sure you don't want something to eat first?"

"No. Nothing. I'm really not hungry, Laura. Thanks anyway."

As we entered the cottage, I asked Amy, "Do you have a light, sort of airy type of dress with you?"

"Yes, why?"

"Let me see it." I followed her to her suitcase, where she pulled out a pink, softly layered, summer dress.

"I wasn't sure if we'd be going out to dinner someplace nice, so I brought this along." She held it in front of her.

"That's perfect! Wear that today."

"Why?"

"Because David is painting a girl in that gazebo up there. And, I think you're the girl. I'm not sure if he is fully aware of it yet, or not. But, that dress will help."

"Okay. I hope so."

"I'm sure so," I smiled.

And I was right. The minute David saw us approaching he walked straight to Amy and enfolded her in his arms. Then he kissed her lovingly, oblivious of my presence. I walked over to the easel and looked at the painting, so they might be alone.

He had detailed the gazebo and added flowers around it. The form within was still faceless. I looked back at David and Amy. He was holding her cherubic face in his hands, as her big, brown eyes sparkled lovingly up at him. Then his arm went around her, and he led her to the gazebo, saying not a word. She sat silently, as he positioned her on the gazebo bench. He tilted her head downward, as he had done mine. But, instead of having her look down at the floor, he asked her to lift her eyes toward him.

"Perfect," he said softly. Then, kissing her, he backed away from the gazebo, not taking his eyes from her.

I could see that there was nothing for me to do, so I made a discreet exit. "I'm going to run into town and pick up some gas and a few things at the store. I'll be back in an hour. The others should be here then, too."

"Okay," mumbled David, his eyes still glued to her, as he painted in Amy's delicate features.

Saying nothing, Amy sat frozen with infatuation, her brown eyes, surrounded with sable lashes, looking lovingly at him.

I returned an hour later. I pulled up behind Bryan's jeep, just as he was getting out.

"Hi, Bryan."

"Hi. Where's Amy?"

"Oh, she's already here. David is painting her in the gazebo."

"Good. That gives us a chance to talk." He leaned up against his jeep, as I came near. "I was going to ask you out tonight, then remembered Amy. What do you think about Amy and David coming with us for dinner and dancing at the Chart House?"

"I'm sure they would enjoy it. Let's go ask them."

"Just a minute. I want to tell you about a dream I had last night. Maybe you can explain it to me."

"Okay, I'll try."

"Well, you and I were in the parking lot at The Chart House. And, we were waiting for someone to bring my car. Then we see a kitten, and I'm worried about it getting hit by the cars. I try to get it, but it runs under a parked car. I look up, to say something to you, and you are gone, and Carol is there. I wonder where Pete is. Then I woke up."

"A parking lot, or a parked car symbolizes stopping and looking at your situation. I'm part of that situation, as are Carol and Pete."

"But what about the kitten? I don't have a kitten. I don't even own a cat."

"A small pet is usually symbolic of a child. A kitten is soft, loving, cuddly, and innocent, just as you remember your child as being when you left her. But, a kitten is also vulnerable, such as shown in the dream by your worrying that the kitten will be hit by a car."

"Does that mean I'm worried about Debby being hit by a car?"

"It's not that literal. It means that you are worried about losing her. You can't seem to get your hands on the kitten. She is just out of reach. And that is your present situation with Debby.

"Then you look up, thinking you will see me. That shows the association you have with me helping you get Debby back. This is in your dream, because I have helped you open up, and do something toward that goal. But, instead of me, you see Carol. This is the realization that Carol stands in the way.

"I can only do so much to help you. I've done that by putting Debby almost within reach. Now I'm gone. Now you must deal with Carol. She is the means of reaching Debby."

"So, why did I dream about Pete?"

"You wonder about Pete, because, for a moment, you think he might present a problem, as well."

"Yeah, that all makes sense. Thanks, Laura."

"To make it even more meaningful to you, write the dream down. Then write about your feelings as you look at each person and object in your dream. For instance, how did you feel, at first, standing in the parking lot?"

"I was waiting for my car. Just waiting. Maybe a little impatient."

"Then, that shows how you are feeling about your situation. You are waiting impatiently. When you look at me, in the dream, are there any feelings or thoughts?"

"Well, it's crazy, but it's like I think you can help find the car. Or, not really find it, but like, you know where it is."

"Okay, remember, when you talk about the car, you are talking about yourself, or the way or means of arriving at a certain goal. You are looking to me to help, because your dream is confirming that I have given you some good advice. Any other feelings or thoughts about me?"

"No. I can't think of any."

"Then, how did you feel about the kitten?"

"Protective...worried about it getting hurt."

"In your dream, you don't want the kitten, your daughter, to get hurt physically. But, you also don't want your daughter to be hurt emotionally. And you are worrying about her being emotionally hurt by you. But right now, she is out of reach...the kitten under the car symbolizes your daughter being out of your reach.

"Now, there is another way of looking at this, besides your wanting to protect your daughter from emotional hurt. We all have male and female in us, right?"

"Yeah, I guess."

"There is the strong, protective masculine side of us. And there is the soft, sensitive, female intuitive side of us. These sides of you are brought out in this dream. They show a subconscious conflict of wanting to be in command, yet feeling vulnerable, like the kitten. This may not be only the conflict about Debby. It might also be an inner conflict about Carol and me."

"That's bullcrap! I don't care about Carol at all!" His eyebrows knit in a deep furrow.

"The fact that you show such emotion when talking about her shows that you do care."

"Yeah. I hate her!"

"Bryan, there is a fine line between hate and love. You loved her once. You could care about her again."

"No. Not after what she did to me."

"Whether it's love or hate, people can't help what they feel…just like you, now. You can't help how you feel. What you are thinking brings out the emotions you feel. What Carol was thinking, when she turned to your friend, Pete, brought out emotions in her. Think about what was going on with the two of you before she left. It might change your mind about it."

"Nothing was going on. I was faithful to her."

"It doesn't have to be something you did. It could be something within her that was not being fulfilled. People often look to others to fill a void they have. They don't realize they can't get what they want from others. They have to work on themselves. When you see her, don't blame Carol or Pete or yourself. Just ask her what was missing in her life at that time. And ask her if she has it now. With no judgment or criticism, just listen to what she says. That should bring you both peace of mind."

"I guess…it might work."

"Let's see what it says in your dream. What were your feelings about Carol when you looked at her in your dream?"

"I was surprised that she was there. I thought it was you at first, but then saw it was Carol."

"This shows your conflicting feelings about us. Did you feel anything about her, or sense or think anything?"

"I didn't feel anything. I just wondered why she was there. Then I wondered where Pete was."

"You may be subconsciously wondering if Pete will show up with Carol and Debby. That's probably bothering you, too."

"Yeah, it is. Damn, I wish I hadn't called her!"

"No you don't. You're just apprehensive. The unknown always worries us. Speaking of the unknown, I wonder where Sam and Mrs. Erickson are." We looked down the road.

"Yeah, here they come," said Bryan. "That's Sam's car, and it looks like Mrs. Erickson is with him."

"I'll go get Amy and David," I said, as I walked around back to the gazebo.

David packed up his paints, while Amy was admiring herself on canvas.

I smiled at Amy and asked, "Isn't he good?"

"He's wonderful!"

"I couldn't have done it without Amy. She's just what I've been waiting for."

In more ways than one, I mused.

David loaded his paints and easel into his van. Then, we entered the open door of the Victorian house.

It was chilly inside, even though the sun was fully overhead. We followed Mrs. Erickson's voice into the ballroom.

"There were happier times here." She looked up at the bare wall above the two fireplaces. "Yes, two portraits should hang here. That was the problem…the portraits…the artist."

I knew now what she meant. David and I had agreed not to tell her or Sam about Anna Marie. We wanted to see what she would come up with on her own. Now, as she spoke of the house, Bryan, David, Amy and I nodded in agreement. She might have read our thoughts. But, I like to think she was reading the story the house was telling her.

We walked into the kitchen. Again, she looked at the door leading to the servant's stairway. She opened the door, and stood just inside of it, as if feeling the energy of the past.

"A young girl would hurry down these stairs to meet her lover out there." She pointed to the backyard. Then she walked over to the back door and unlocked it. Opening it, she walked out onto the expansive back porch, then down the steps to what had been the garden. We followed quietly, keeping within reach of her voice.

Walking toward the gazebo, chills went up my back and into my hairline. I didn't know if it was from the cool, sea breeze, or from the excitement of Amy and David's new love. Or possibly it was from my apprehension of the unfolding mystery. I hoped Mrs. Erickson could fill in the missing pieces of the story. This thought charged me with excitement, as I scooted closely along behind her.

Mrs. Erickson stood looking inside of the gazebo. "She sat here, as the young man painted her."

I wondered if she was confusing the recent vibrations of Amy and David, with Elizabeth and Simon. I looked at Amy and David. He had his arm around Amy, smiling down at her.

Then Mrs. Erickson looked up at the house. "The middle room upstairs…she watched and waited for him there. Then down the back stairs to here." She turned and looked down the rickety steps. "Sometimes…down there…late at night."

Then she looked out to the dock. "Her father came on a ship. The boy is gone. She watches and waits for him here…and there." She motioned to the gazebo.

Then she led us back to the house. As we walked past the forlorn, forgotten garden, Mrs. Erickson said, "Later…it was the garden that captivated her attention. She set her mind to tending to the flowers."

We walked back into the kitchen, and up the servant's stairway to the second floor. She looked into the room, which was carpeted and newly painted.

"The children play here. But, that was later. Not part of her family. A new family lived here with little children. They were happy for a while."

We walked into the next room. "The mother of the children is unhappy here. *Too cold!* She says. The father agrees to go."

Mrs. Erickson walked over to the fireplace in this bedroom, and placed her hand on the mantle. "The Captain died here. This was his room. He was angry when he died. A relentlessly angry, tired old man. Not so old in years, but in mind and temperament. Something wrong with his arm…something between the arm and the heart."

I looked at Bryan and smiled. He raised one eyebrow in recognition of what I was thinking. Then, we walked into the room across the hall.

"This was the older sister. She was strong like her father, the captain. Obedient and commanding, she ran things in the house. She was also protective. She took care of the younger one. Yes, she took care of the house, and the younger one took care of the garden."

Mrs. Erickson stood silently as if listening, or waiting to hear something else. "So much anger in this room." Then she turned. "Okay, let's go into the next room."

I now knew that the next room was Elizabeth's. This was the room where I felt a hand touch my back. This was the only room in which I had felt any energy. The room was cool, except where the sun reflected off of the veranda and through the glass panels of the French doors. I had a compulsion to go over and stand in the sunlight, to warm up, but thought I should stay behind Mrs. Erickson to let her guide the way.

She stood in the middle of the room, slowly turning, like a manikin on a pedestal. She seemed to be seeing the various parts of the room as they had been lived in decades ago.

"The younger one was ill. Not ill, but confined to her bed. There was a loss. The baby was taken away from her. She grieved for it. The baby lived, but was taken away."

She faced the window. "This is where she watched for the young man. She grieved here, too."

Mrs. Erickson stood looking out of the window, just as I had. Had I felt those same feelings that Mrs. Erickson now was feeling? But, I didn't recognize them. I hadn't read what the energy in the room was trying to tell me.

"The boy never came back. She waited and watched. But, he never came back."

Then she turned abruptly toward the bedroom door. "There is something upstairs." She looked at the ceiling. "Up there."

We followed her out of the bedroom and down the hall to the attic door. Chills were flashing up my back, as Sam unlocked the attic door. David and Amy eagerly followed Sam and Mrs. Erickson up the attic steps. I wanted to stay back. I felt like going back downstairs and out of the front door into the sunlight. My whole body was shaking with chills. I could feel every hair on my arms standing on end.

Bryan sensed my reluctance, so he stood by the door, waiting for me to move. Finally, he reached his hand out and pulled me up the steps with him. Once in motion, I quickly ascended the bare wooden steps.

The attic was old and musty smelling. I had the feeling as if I were acting in a production of *Arsenic and Old Lace*. From what I could see of the attic, it was empty. Eight dormer windows, four cut into each side of the roof, threw filmy rays of sunlight on the dusty wooden floor.

"There is something here. We must look for it. It's important that we find it," Mrs. Erickson told us.

We all started scanning the crannies and crevices of the attic. I made sure I stayed close to Bryan, because that feeling of wariness still hadn't left me.

"Do you think we'll find a body?" Bryan whispered to me, as we approached a dark, cobwebbed corner.

"Bryan! You could have gone all day without saying that!" I reprimanded him.

"Just kidding. There's such an air of mystery in here, it just seemed to need a little lightening up. Besides, a hundred year old body would be decomposed into fragments by now."

"Is that what you think it is?" I scrutinized him with a wide-eyed stare.

"Well, they don't know what happened to the artist. He might have been murdered by the captain, and stashed up here."

I gulped and said nothing, just hung onto Bryan's arm, as if some apparition might come out of the dark and attack me.

David and Amy were already coming back from the other end of the attic. "Nothing down there but dust and cobwebs," David called to us.

Sam was watching Mrs. Erickson, as she walked to a dormer window. She leaned down and looked out of the window facing the backyard. She stood there for a while, then straightened and looked toward us.

"Yes," she said, somewhat to herself. "This window is just above the young lady's room. The gazebo can be seen from it. I must concentrate in this area." She slowly moved out from the window, her hands lightly touching the rafter as she walked. She stopped at the center of the room, and walked back, still connecting with the ceiling. She did this repeatedly, going from beam to beam, until she stopped in a dark corner, where a beam met the floor.

"Here...it is here," she said in a solemnly mysterious voice.

Again, chills shot up my spine, as I envisioned her pulling a skeleton out of the dark, dusty recesses of the rafters.

She cautiously followed the beam to the floor, and felt behind it, where a supporting wall jutted out. I think I was really more afraid of her connecting with a mouse or spider, than a corpse.

"Yes, there is something here." She was on her knees, reaching between the beam and the wall. Carefully, she brought out a brownish looking tube, tied closed with a cord. Sam helped her up. And Bryan took the tube from her hand.

"It looks like some kind of parchment. Maybe it's a legal document." Bryan turned to show it to the rest of us.

"Maybe it's a will," I said.

"Or...you don't suppose it's a marriage certificate?" Amy added

"Let me see, Bryan." David reached for it. "I think I know what it is. Let's get some light on it." We followed him to a window. "Yes," he said. "We can't open this."

"Why not?" Amy and I chorused.

"Because it's canvas. And it's very old. And it would crumble into pieces if we tried to prey it open."

"What do we do then?" Amy asked.

"There are places that restore old documents and paintings. I can find out from the museum in town, or if they don't know someone, I'll call the Fine Arts Museum in San Francisco, and see if they can help us."

"What do you think it is, Mrs. Erickson?" I asked.

Mrs. Erickson put her hands on the tube. "It's a painting of her… in the gazebo. She hid it."

"I suppose, when the captain found out his daughter was pregnant, he stormed out of the house to confront the artist. And Elizabeth knew he would destroy her portrait. So she hid it up here." I conjectured.

"Yeah," David agreed. "She cut the canvas off the frame, and rolled it up, so it could be hidden."

"And she tied it with her hair ribbon," added Mrs. Erickson.

"Then, Annabelle, seeing her sister's portrait gone, thought the captain had cut it up, and thought he might do the same to hers, so she hid hers, probably in her room," I added.

"Out of sight, out of mind," added Bryan. "Maybe he searched and gave up. Or maybe he didn't care, as long as the paintings weren't around where he could see them."

"Sister Ignatius told us that after the captain's death, Annabelle must have brought her painting out. Or maybe the nuns found it in her room," I said.

"Or," said Bryan, "maybe after Annabelle's death, Elizabeth found Annabelle's painting. Maybe, at that age, she couldn't remember where hers was."

We all looked at Mrs. Erickson.

"She wanted us to know about it. It was something that has bothered her all of these years," said Mrs. Erickson. "The other residents, who acquired this house, didn't understand. She tried to communicate with them, but they didn't understand. They grew fearful of the house, and left."

Talking about ghosts didn't bother me now. No more chills. For some unspoken reason, I felt comfortable now. Was it all in my head? Had my fears and apprehensions fabricated the intense atmosphere? Or had the house settled down now? Was Elizabeth happy now?

As we walked down the two flights of stairs, everything seemed peaceful in the house. It seemed warmer. Or was it my imagination? It could have been coming from the cold, dark attic into the sunshine that changed my perspective. But the house did seem much happier and friendlier. The mind can play funny tricks.

Chapter 14

Connections

When we first meet people, we attempt to find some link between them and ourselves. As we ask them questions, and tell them the better parts about us, we unconsciously become connected to them in ways that make them an integral part of our being. Once absorbed into each other's experience, we will never be the same. For now, those connections have been imprinted upon our lives, whether we connect with them again, or not.

That night, David and Bryan took Amy and me out to the Chart House for dinner. She looked fresh and bright in the pink, pastel flowered dress in which David had painted her. The entire evening, David could barely take his eyes off Amy. She glowed, both from happiness, and from the bronze tan she had acquired from lying on the deck chaise that afternoon. Brown curls cascaded around the petite dimpled face. Big brown eyes glistened with love, as Egyptian-fan lashes swooped slowly past them.

Everything was new and exciting to her. She was delighted with the quaint elegance of the Chart House - the sailor-suited waitresses, the jug menu, and the rowboat salad bar. I remembered how fascinated I was at first seeing it, but there was something different in watching Amy. Her spellbound excitement seemed to absorb the entire environment into all of her senses…and David's enchantment along with it.

As we slowly consumed our dinners of various courses with steak and lobster, we became further acquainted and connected by a consistently animated conversation. We talked about the Victorian house, the captain, the MacLean sisters, the nuns, and the young portrait artist. We talked about Mrs. Erickson's talent and about various forms of extra-sensory perception, ghosts and spirit communication. We talked about our lives and the places we had lived. We played an equal part in engrossing ourselves in each other's lives.

When we moved into the cocktail lounge, I felt an instant shift in the atmosphere. While the restaurant gave one the feeling of being on the deck of a cruise ship, the lounge transported us to a tropical island. The bar area was topped with a palm leaf roof. Waitresses wore colorful, wrap-around Hawaiian sarongs. And the men wore Hawaiian print shirts with khaki pants.

There was a small combo of a lovely, young blonde girl, who sang and played a tambourine; a young black man, who also sang and played several percussion instruments; and an Asian young man, who made a spinet and a synthesizer sound like a five-piece band.

We ordered drinks, and David and Amy immediately got up to dance. They spent the majority of the evening in each other's arms, swaying to the music. While they danced, Bryan talked, both apprehensively and enthusiastically about seeing his eleven-year-old daughter, Debby and his ex-wife, Carol.

"I'm anxious to see Debby, but I'm worried about how she feels about me. She might think I deserted her. I don't know what Carol has told her about me. I don't know how Carol feels about me now…"

As he talked about Carol, I was reminded about the dreams I had about my relationship with Bryan. The roadblock dream told me to stop and look around. The mountain dream showed Bryan balancing his feelings about Carol and me. The island dream, with the Victorian house, showed our relationship as insecure, and that I should stick to my Victorian principles. Then, the lost purse dream, again, showing me the insecurity of our relationship.

Amy stayed with me Wednesday and Thursday; but she had to get back to San Francisco on Friday to work at the pizza place on the weekend.

The following weekend Amy took off work, so she could bring her mother and father to see the Victorian house, and to meet David. Amy phoned me ahead to ask if she could stay with me, while her parents stayed at the motel in Milton.

Bryan, David, Amy and I took Anna and Harold to The Chart House. Amy had confided in me that she wanted her parents to fall in love with the area, the house and David, just as she had. We had a great meal and great conversation, with lots of laughs. Anna and Harold were friendly and fun.

Amy encouraged Bryan and David to talk about the local people, jobs, history and economy. None of us knew what was on her mind, except David.

We had ridden there in David's van, which held a hint of paint and turpentine. David dropped Anna and Harold off at the Motel in Milton. Then we took Bryan home. On the way to the beach cottage, David and Amy told me their plan.

"Laura, I didn't have a chance to tell you earlier, but David and I have a plan for the Victorian house."

"Oh, really? What is it?"

"We want to buy it and live in it," she smiled.

"How nice!" I smiled at them. Ten years ago I would have said, *Oh, how nice, you're getting married!* But, these days so many young people live together, have a baby, *then* get married. So *how nice* sufficed.

"We can do a lot of the work on it before the summer's over… before David goes back to teaching full time. I can help him sand, paint and paper. And he can help me design and put in the gardens, lawns and pathways. Then, we'll open it to the public."

I must have looked surprised, because she gave a quick laugh and continued.

"The parlor off of the dining room will be the boutique. We can sell David's paintings, and he can do some small things like stationery, miniatures and paint pottery. The ballroom will be a tearoom, with tables and chairs, to serve sandwiches, cookies, cakes, tea, coffee and soft drinks.

"And I will maintain a nursery on the grounds, where I'll sell plants all year round. Also, I can make flower arrangements – fresh and dried, and grapevine wreaths and baskets, and other things to sell in the shop."

"That sounds wonderful, Amy! A lot of work, but you both have the energy to do it. I know it will be a success."

"We could have it ready in two months," David added.

"Not the gardens," said Amy. "It will take longer for them to come to full maturity. But it will be a start."

"Right!" said David. "We'll start on a small scale, just advertise in Milton and Northport at first."

"Sure," said Amy. "We don't want to be too overwhelmed at first."

"And we'll hire high school kids to help serve the food and work in the kitchen. We can get them pretty cheap. And eventually they will man the store and nursery, and Amy and I will just float around seeing that it all runs smoothly."

"And, Laura, we could even rent rooms, or have a Bed and Breakfast in the summer when people are traveling through."

"That's wonderful, Amy! Have you told your parents about it?" I was sure she hadn't told them, because nothing was said about it at dinner.

"Not yet. I want them to see the house first and fall in love with it like I did. And Milton too. In the morning David is going to pick us up and take us all around the county, to see the sights. You can come too, if you want. Then we meet Sam at the house at two."

"Thanks, but I don't want to be a fifth wheel."

"No, Laura," said David. "You won't be. Maybe you can help us convince them of our plan."

"Yes, Laura. You have to come."

"Thanks, I'd like to come. So, I suppose you have figured out how you're going to finance this plan?"

"Yeah, well, David has a lot of money saved. I don't have any. But, if I can convince Mom and Dad on the idea, I think they'll pay my part of the down payment."

"Yeah, we'll both put in half for the down payment and escrow fees and stuff. And I can handle the monthly payments and food."

"Yes, and I'll take out a business loan to develop the nursery and gardens. In the evenings David and I can make things to sell in the boutique. When we get enough things made to sell, we'll have a Sunday open house and serve just coffee, tea, cookies and nut bread, to make it easy. We can do that just on Sundays at first, to see how it goes."

"Yeah, and as we get better at it, we'll advertise in the San Francisco newspapers."

"That sounds like a great plan. And I know you'll succeed. You both have the energy and creativity to make it work."

"We also thought of having large cans of soup ready, in case we have a big crowd and need more food," said David.

"Yes," said Amy. "And I can make soups and salads, when the garden is producing. I can also make a small cookbook of my recipes to sell in our boutique. And David can illustrate it. And I'll make jam with our berries, and sell it in cute little jars."

"Wow, it sounds like you have an infinite number of ideas for this venture. I know it will work if your enthusiasm continues as it is now."

"It will. I love working with plants. And I have always wanted to have an old Victorian house to fix up."

"Yeah, me too," said David. "I like to build and restore old things. My minor was in industrial arts, so I can do most of the building and repair work on the place. We want to bring it back to how it looked originally."

"We're going to see about getting some of the furniture back from the convent, even if we have to buy it back. It's important to me, not just because it belonged to my ancestors, but because it belongs to the house. I want the house to be happy again. It's sad now, and I know

I can make it happy again, with David's help." She smiled lovingly at David.

"I know you can, too," I agreed. Then I climbed out of the van and went inside the beach house, so Amy and David could say goodnight.

When Amy came in, we talked long into the night about her ideas. She drew pictures, diagraming the gardens she wanted to develop, and showed me where the nursery greenhouse would be built. She planned to have flowers to sell all year round.

She said David wanted to rebuild the carriage house, and find a vintage carriage to display there for tourists. He also wanted to rebuild the steps leading down to the beach, so people could come up from the beach to enjoy the place, and David could go down to paint.

Such wonderful plans, I thought. *And, only one thing standing in their way… Anna and Harold. Their support was needed to buy the house.* The next day, David picked up Amy and me. Then we drove to Milton to pick up Amy's parents for our drive around the countryside.

"Laura, please don't say anything to my parents about our plans to buy the house. We want them to see it first."

"Of course not. I'll follow your lead."

As we ventured through the countryside, I looked at it with new eyes. I thought of Anna and Harold and tried to get inside their minds, to see it as they might see it…rolling hills, trees, vineyards, flowers and farms. Was it attractive? Interesting? Enticing? Unique? Different from where they lived? Is it a captivating enough area to entice them to want to come back, and to have their daughter living here?

David drove us to the redwood forest, where the tallest trees in the world are. We walked along the path through the dense forest of gigantic trees, ferns and wild flowers. Then we visited the gift shop, where we all bought souvenirs.

We drove back along the coast. Birds, boats, beachcombers and quaint little beach cottages mesmerized us. We stopped at a restaurant, overlooking the beach, and had lunch. The beach was vibrant with activity, as people enjoyed the sand and surf, and seals popped their heads up to watch. Anna and Harold seemed to be delighted with it all.

David and Amy were so excited for her parents to see the MacLean house, we arrived there before two o' clock. As we parked in front of it, Anna said, "My, it is austere, isn't it?"

And Harold said, "Yeah, it looks like a haunted house. Are you sure there aren't ghosts living here?"

"No, I'm not sure, Dad," Amy said with a smile and a twinkle in her eye, as if hoping that there were.

We all laughed. Except Harold, who grumbled, "We're 20 minutes early. What are we going to do, just sit here?"

"No, Dad. I'm going to show you around the outside. Come on."

We all got out of the van, and Amy led the way, as the irascible iron-gate squawked its intolerance of us. We followed Amy on the red brick pathway along side of the house. Amy chattered incessantly about what had been planted here and what needed to be done there.

"Can't you just imagine this rose garden all in bloom, Mom? With a grape arbor over there, and trellis here covered with climbing miniature roses?"

Anna mumbled approval between Amy's animated patter. Harold remained silent. We all wondered what he thought, or whether he cared at all.

"And this is where great-grandma Elizabeth would sneak out to meet her lover, the artist." Amy headed toward the gazebo. "It was covered in purple wisteria...very fragrant blooms. He painted her here."

We all looked inside the gazebo, gazing in a subconscious effort to visualize Elizabeth posing for her portrait.

"And they made love here, too." Amy said this in a most reverent tone.

Anna and Harold suddenly pulled their heads out and stepped back, as if intruding on someone's privacy. Harold frowned and walked toward the cliff-side fence.

Anna scolded Amy, "Amy, you shouldn't talk like that. What will people think?"

"Oh, Mom, don't be so Victorian. That's what caused all of the trouble for great-grandma in the first place."

I could see that there would be much difficulty in convincing Anna and Harold to let Amy move into this house with David. I wondered if I would be able to help at all.

As we stood on the cliff, looking out toward the sea, Amy told about the big cargo ships pulling into the dock. A cooling sea breeze played with our hair, and teased our dresses into dancing lightly around our legs. A peaceful enchantment enveloped the atmosphere, so that, even as we three women walked away, Harold and David remained, silently staring out to sea.

David told Amy and me later that Harold had confided in him that he had always wanted to sail around the world. However, once settled down with a family, those notions faded. But he still liked looking out at the ocean and dreaming about it.

"I guess we men have a natural sense of adventure in us," David told him.

"Yeah, you're right," Harold agreed. "And if you don't satisfy that sense of adventure, in some way, life becomes a drag. You drag yourself to work and you drag yourself back home. A person needs something to look forward to, something to be striving for, besides just the 9 to 5."

"I know what you mean, Mr. Burns," David replied. "Sometimes I feel that at school, though God knows there's plenty of challenge there! But when I'm working on a painting, I hurry home with all kinds of enthusiasm to get back to it."

"God! I wish I had something like that in my life!" Harold frowned at the expanse of azure sea.

"Don't you do any traveling or sightseeing?"

"No. We used to when the kids were little. But they started going their own way, and we just settled into a routine of work and TV. And that's it."

David told us he couldn't think of anything else to reply. But, I began thinking that maybe this project of the house might be the adventure that Anna and Harold needed.

We were standing on the back porch, peeking in the windows, when Sam found us. David and Amy had told Sam about their plan. They told him not to say anything about it to her parents until after they saw the house. In the meantime, Amy had told her parents that Sam would probably try to sell the house to them, because he was very anxious to sell it.

"Didn't you tell him that we're just looking at it because it was owned by your family?" Harold asked.

"Yeah, I did, Dad. But it's been on the market a long time now, and he'll do his best to try to talk you into it."

"He can save his breath. We're not movin'," growled Harold.

Amy smiled at David, completely undaunted. David raised his eyebrows, a bit uncertainly.

As we walked through the house, I opened windows and doors to let the fresh sea breeze in. Amy related what Mrs. Erickson had said in each room, filling in and developing the story in its entirety, just as if they were tourists roaming through an ancient castle. Her mother followed along side of her, listening intently.

Harold strolled independently around the rooms, caressing the natural wood shelves and casings, and staring silently out of the multi-paneled windows, as if uniting himself with the house and its incredible view.

Sam followed Harold, interjecting a few phrases between Amy's enthusiastic patter. "Fine wood…well taken care of…all original windows…good seal. Sound walls. The Catholics upgraded the plumbing and remodeled the bathroom in the late 70's. The present owners had a new heating system put in, and all new electrical, because that was pretty old."

And as Harold looked out of the windows, Sam said, "Great view! You can see ships passing here from San Francisco to Seattle. And on the other side you can see the mountains. Nice neighborhood... friendly and quiet. Lots of retired people around here." Sam knew his job well.

David and I were sort of oscillating between Amy and Sam, trying to hear what they were saying, and trying to judge Anna's and Harold's receptivity.

"My, it sure has a lot of bedrooms!" Anna exclaimed. "And a view from each one. On one side the ocean and the other side the mountains. It's lovely!"

"Yes, Mother." Amy was getting more serious now, calling her mom *mother.* I stayed within earshot of them, listening intently.

"A person could buy this house and rent out the rooms to help pay for it."

"Yes, I suppose so," Anna agreed.

"It has been on the market a long time, and the owners are really anxious to sell it. A person could get a really good deal on it."

"Why hasn't it sold? It seems to be a sound house."

"Mom, I think it was because of the spirits," Amy whispered.

Anna looked surprised. "Look, Amy, it's one thing talking about the history of the house, and a medium sensing what has taken place here, but it's entirely another thing to say it's haunted by ghosts. I'm surprised you believe such things, let alone other people who stay away from the house because of an old wives' tale. You don't believe that, do you?"

"Mom, when I first walked through this house, cold chills went right through me."

"Oh, Amy, that was just your imagination."

"No, Mom. It was as if a cold, clammy presence was standing next to me. And there was something unsettling about the house, as if it wanted to tell us something."

"Amy, you've been seeing too many weird shows. Your imagination is working overtime. I don't feel a thing in here. It's a very pleasant house."

"Right! It is now. But before we found the painting in the attic, Elizabeth's spirit was here trying to tell us about it. Now she's satisfied and she's gone."

"Oh, Amy, really!"

"Well, you don't have to believe it, Mom. But there was something ominous that kept people from buying it. And now that the house feels okay, someone is going to snatch it up fast, because the price is so low right now."

"Probably so," Anna agreed.

"Don't you think $60,000 is a steal for this house and all of this property, and the view and everything?"

"Yes, it is." Anna looked questioningly at Amy's enthusiasm.

"Mom, I want to buy it. It's our house. It was my great-grandma's house. I want to live here." She whispered this, not wanting to tell her dad until her mom was convinced.

"Amy, we can't move. We have our jobs in San Raphael," she whispered back.

"No, Mom. I don't mean you… and Dad. I mean me."

"Amy, you don't have any money, or even a good job. And we can't afford to support you. Let's be practical."

"I am, Mom. I've thought it over very carefully. David and I want to go into business together."

"What kind of business?"

"This house. It would be our business. We'd fix it up to show. We'd have a boutique, an art gallery, a tearoom, and a B & B, or just rent rooms year round."

"You and David? Are you talking about marriage?" She whispered.

"Well, no. Not right now, anyway. Just a partnership."

"Amy, you mean you'd both live here in this house?" Anna kept her voice low so Harold wouldn't hear her.

"Well, yes, but in different rooms. That way we could work on it, and rent the other rooms out. David could paint, and I could bring back the gardens with plants from home. He wants to rebuild that old shed in the back, and make it into a nursery, where I could sell plants and flowers."

"But Amy, where do you plan on getting the money for all of this?"

"It would be a partnership, 50-50. David has enough money saved up for his part of the down payment. And his income from teaching and selling his paintings will support the renovation. And we can get a grant from the government for fixing up a historical place."

"And what about your part of it?"

"Well, I'll look for a job in town. And I can sell some of the wreaths and things I've made…"

"And your part of the down payment?"

"I was hoping to borrow it from you. And I'll pay you back as my business increases. And, once I get a job, I can take out a loan from the bank. I know it will work. David is as excited as I am about this. We both love this house. And he is a hard worker and talented too."

"I'm sure he is, Amy. But what are people going to think about you living here with him? It's obvious that you like each other more than just business partners."

"I know." Amy blushed. "But, honestly Mom, we'll have our own rooms, and there will be other people living here too. And really, Mom, let's face it. If I'm going to do something, I could do it anywhere with him. Living together doesn't mean that we're sleeping together, any more than not living together means we aren't. Right Laura?"

"Right," I smiled. "Look at Elizabeth and Simon."

"Yeah. It's those prudish Victorian principles that caused all of the trouble with them. If her dad had been more understanding, she would have married the artist, and we would probably already be living here."

Anna was overwhelmed by this sudden rush of new ideas. She blinked incredulously, and I could see her backing off, not ready to make a decision quite yet. Sam and Harold were coming toward us. So I thought I'd better help both Amy and Anna out.

"Amy, let's go to the beach house and we'll all talk about it there, where we can relax." I said this softly, looking at them both for approval.

"Shall we ask Sam to come?" Amy asked me.

"No, he would put pressure on your dad, and he has enough pressure with you." I smiled, and they both gave an embarrassed laugh.

"Well, I guess we've seen everything," said Harold. "Are you ready to go?" He asked Anna.

Sam looked questioningly at Amy. She lagged behind to tell him that she would phone him later. I walked out with Anna, and David walked with Harold, pointing out where the carriage house had stood.

We said thank you to Sam, and David drove us to my place. I put on a pot of coffee, and cut up some coffee cake I'd bought in town. Then I joined the others on the deck.

"It must be very peaceful living at the beach," Anna said to me, as we looked out at the serenity of the sea.

"Yes, it is. No sirens or honking cars. And, not many visitors either. Just the rolling of the waves and the seagulls, with a continuously changing panorama of color as the sun moves across the sky."

"And, it's even prettier from up there." Amy pointed toward the cliff.

"Yes, and it's peaceful up there too," Anna agreed. "That's the house over there, isn't it?"

"Yes. See that old wooden stairway? David says he can rebuild those steps."

Harold heard Amy. "Oh, are you interested in buying the place, David?" He asked.

Amy looked surprised, suddenly realizing she had let the cat out of the bag. David looked embarrassed, as his eyes darted from Amy to Harold to me. "Yes, Sir. I do want to buy it." He didn't want to say anymore until Amy was ready.

"I suppose an artist needs lots of room to paint," Harold continued.

"Yes, uh, it's pretty messy work. I like to spread out. The attic would make a great art studio. It's well insolated, no leaks. I could give private lessons there, and have a weekly art class."

"I guess you'd have to have a couple of incomes to support that house." Harold was referring to David's teaching at the high school as well as giving private lessons.

I could see that David felt put on the spot. I was sure he wished that Amy would say something. But she remained silent, wearing a frozen smile.

"Yeah, the high school and private lessons, and private classes, and selling my art. And I have quite a bit of money saved up, because I knew I'd want to buy a house someday. That's a good house. It's in good condition and a good investment. But there are things I'd want to do with it, like paint and wallpaper, and rebuild that old carriage house. There are pictures at the convent that show how it looked."

By this time, Amy was bursting. She wanted to tell her dad about all of their exciting plans. But she knew her dad too well. He always said *no* before he said *yes*. She wanted to present this idea to him so subtly that he wouldn't realize he was being led into it.

"Yes, Dad," Amy blurted out excitedly, "I thought that tomorrow we'd drive out to the convent, and see the pictures and furniture that came from the house. Sister Ignatius said it is ours."

"Look, Amy," her dad admonished. "We don't have room for a bunch of old furniture at our house."

"I don't mean for our house, Dad. That furniture belongs in Great-grandma Elizabeth's house. It must be taken there."

Harold looked from Amy to David, and asked, "Is that what you had in mind?"

"Yes, Sir. We want to fix the house up just the way it was. We can get a government grant to restore it."

"What do you mean *we*?" Who is *we?*" Harold asked suspiciously.

David looked helplessly at Amy. Amy immediately jumped in with both feet.

"Dad, I'm going to help David."

"That's impossible! It's too far away. You've got to get a job in San Raphael and start supporting yourself."

"I will start supporting myself. But I'm going to do it here. I'm going to start a nursery here in Milton. I'll develop it out of the old gardener's shed up there. There are no nurseries in this area, so I'll have a corner on the market. And I can sell my crafts too."

"And where will you live?"

"Here, in great-grandma's house."

"With this boy? No, you're not, Amy! You're not going to move up here and live with this boy!"

"Dad, you sound just like the captain. Now I know how Elizabeth felt. We are just going to set up a partnership, Dad. That's all."

"In my day they called it marriage. Today they call it setting up a partnership," he growled at her.

"No, Dad, it's not that way. We want to buy the house together and make a business out of it. We'll have a tearoom, a nursery, a crafts shop, an art gallery, and we'll rent rooms."

"Forget it! My daughter's not going to come here and move in with someone she's only known for one week. No offense, boy. I like you. You're a good kid. But Amy's only 24, and she's a good girl, and…"

"Right! I'm 24 and that makes me an adult. I'm old enough to live my own life the way I see fit. And I am a good girl, and mature enough to know what I want."

David could see that Amy had her dad in a corner. And a man's honor was at stake here…both his and Harold's. So he stepped in, to try to soften things for both of them.

"Sir, I asked Amy to marry me, and she said no. We do love each other, but she wants the house to be perfect so we can be married there…with the flowers in bloom. You're right, we've only known each other a week, but we know that we're right for each other. And, by setting up a partnership in writing, we can be sure of our love and making a go of the house. If either doesn't work out, we can buy the other out. If it does work out, we'll be married in June."

"It isn't right…her living here with you," Harold feebly croaked.

"Sir, I intend to make the attic my home. The furniture I have now will all go up there. It will be my apartment and my studio. There's plenty of room up there for me…like a French artist living in a Parisian loft in Montmartre."

"And I'll live downstairs," Amy added. "And we'll rent the other rooms to supplement our income."

"Yeah, with my job teaching at the high school, giving art lessons, and the government grant for restoration, we should do okay."

"And the gardener's shed will make a great nursery office for me," added Amy. "I'll propagate and sell plants there."

Anna could see that Harold was softening, so she stepped in to help out. "It sounds like you two have this all planned out. But, Amy, it sounds to me like David would be supporting the whole operation. Where's your money coming from? It will take a while before the nursery is off the ground. Don't you have to put money into the house too?"

"Well…yes. I can't take out a bank loan until I have a job, but if I could get a loan from you for the down payment on the house, I could start paying you back when we rent the rooms." She looked back and forth from her mom to her dad.

Harold didn't give in easily. He wanted the privilege of thinking about it before he committed himself totally. He looked at Anna. She was smiling confidently at him. "Well, your mom and I will talk about it."

To Amy, that meant yes. And she knew she would be contacting Sam the next day.

As we had coffee and cake, Amy expostulated further about the many things she and David were planning. Harold and Anna asked questions and gave suggestions, which made David know that all would be well.

Watching Harold, I could see that spark of enthusiasm gradually relenting, and breaking through the rich soil of Mother Nature, until it was in full bloom, offering its service toward the MacLean renovation.

As they left, Harold, Anna, David and Amy talked excitedly about seeing the items that were at the convent. They decided to drive to the convent right then. It was 4 o' clock, still early enough before dinner.

I stayed home and curled up with a good book. By the time Amy came in, I had fallen asleep on the couch. She had lost no enthusiasm as she sat down and excitedly told me about the things she saw at the convent.

"Mother Bernadette let us read the letter from Sister Mary Angelica, about the MacLean family, and our inheritance. Mother Bernadette recommended that we drive Sister Ignatius up from San Francisco, so she can give us the specific items that came from the house. Mom and Dad said they'd bring her up. And they told us to call Sam tomorrow and we'd all talk about buying the house. Mom and Dad are going to cosign for us, so I guess that makes them partners too. We need them to cosign because David and I don't own property, or have any collateral.

"David has a friend with a truck, who'll help us move. What little I have at my folk's place can be brought up by car. Sam's going to ask the owners, once we're approved, if we can move right in."

She was so excited. I could see why her parents relented so easily. They wanted to help their daughter in her new career. And even though they were hesitant at first about the circumstances, there was an eternal connection between them that must not be broken. They also understood the connection that Amy had with David…and the house.

Chapter 15

Reflections

When Bryan's ex-wife, Carol, and their eleven-year-old daughter, Debby, arrived in Milton, I hardly heard from Bryan. That was understandable. When he did call to try to sandwich me in to meet them before they left, I told him to concentrate on them right now. I would meet them on another visit. No use in complicating things. He sounded confused, but somewhat relieved. He also said that Carol was divorced from Pete. He sounded relieved about that, as well.

Amy came and stayed with me each weekend, bringing carloads of her stuff to store at my place until she was allowed to move into the MacLean house. She and David cleaned it from top to bottom. Then the move-in weekend was a blockbuster. Amy brought two girlfriends from San Francisco to help with the move. And David had his friend with the truck, and four high school boys to help move.

Anna and Harold brought Sister Ignatius up from San Francisco, and they all three stayed at the convent of St. James. Anna and Harold enjoyed it thoroughly. They were given presidential treatment.

"And the food sure is good there!" Harold exclaimed.

"The nuns won Harold over," said Anna. "I think he'll start going to church with me now."

All of us, including Anna and Harold, moved furniture and personal items from the convent and from David's apartment, and we unloaded Amy's car.

The whole gang of us had the first meal in the house at the old oak dining room table, part of the museum items which Vivian had given them. It was pizza on paper plates. Harold and Anna seemed to be almost as excited as David and Amy were. They talked about taking a week off of work and coming up to help them with the gardening and painting. The light of enthusiasm was bright in Harold's eyes as he planned with David how he could help.

It was shortly after that when I began taking long drives along the coast and into the hills and valleys of the wine country. I needed to get away and discover new vistas. The beach still held an exciting fascination for me, with its powerfully crashing waves, roaring and rolling in continuous commotion. The subtle complexity of the evolutionary flow of life - above, below and among its sand and surf was captivating.

I marveled at the contrasting solemnity of sky meeting sea in a crimson glow of golden enchantment. I loved these magnetic changes in the atmosphere, which grasped my senses, and elevated my awareness of the interrelatedness of the universe.

I sat on my deck for long periods of time, filling my senses with sights, sounds and smells of ocean and beach. But, within me was unrest. Summer was ending, and the time had arrived to make plans for my future.

Driving through the countryside, I felt good about myself. There seemed to be a new me, self-confident, happy, self-reliant and open to new challenges. I had stopped dwelling on my shortcomings and inadequacies. Now I looked forward to new opportunities.

This change in attitude came partly from being in a new environment, and partly from being part of Amy's and David's experience. The enthusiasm and excitement for a new adventure, which I saw in Amy, David, Anna and Harold, was contagious. I loved it. I started searching for my own special place.

I knew I wanted to live close to the ocean and close to the mountains, but away from the traffic and tourism. It had to be near a mental facility, where I could work, but a small place with no congestion…a place of simplicity.

I researched mental facilities on the northern coast of California. There was one near the town of Brookfield, which was an hour's drive from the coast. I visited it and liked what I saw. Talking to the head administrator there, I discovered they had an opening for me. I filled out necessary paperwork, and left…leaving my options open to change my mind, if needed.

Brookfield was a college town, small, but lively. It bubbled with activity. I liked it, but decided to explore the hills and dells surrounding it. About thirty miles away I discovered a small, sequestered valley, where a tiny town lay between rolling hills. The town was called Elmsville.

As I drove through its small streets of tree-lined houses, I saw a white stucco cottage, which reminded me of my grandparent's small house in San Clemente. A sign in front of it said, *For Sale By Owner.*

I wasn't in the market for a house. Nor was I sure I wanted to live in this town. But something compelled me, like the same mysterious force that made me want to find out more about the house on the cliff.

Not at all like the majestic, Victorian square brick structure on the cliff, this cottage was small and unimposing. White stucco exterior, with wooden windowsills and doors, and red tile roof and chimney, reminded me of the small homes that were built in the 1940s in Southern California. They tied in with the twenty-one coastal Missions built by Padre Serra in the 1600s.

It was more curiosity than sense that lead me up the cement walk to the door. I knocked, and a grey-haired, heavy-set lady opened the door.

"Hi. I'm Laura Christopher, and I saw your sign out front…"

"Oh, come in. I'll show you the house." She seemed very friendly and eager to tell me about the house.

"Well, I was just exploring the area. I'm not sure I'm even ready to buy a house. But I love the looks of your house. It reminds me of my grandparent's house in San Clemente."

"Oh, let me show you around. It was built by a Swedish contractor in the 1940s, shortly after the war. There were a lot of young couples needing housing at that time. It's small, but very well built. They don't make them like this anymore. There is one bedroom and one bath. And the garage is separate from the house."

Now I knew why I liked this place so much. My Swedish grandfather was a builder. He built a 1940s cottage for my grandmother in San Clemente, California, near San Diego.

We walked into the living room. A small fireplace was on the wall to our right. It had bookshelves on each side of it. Windows looked out to the front and the side. It was very peaceful. Her furniture looked like it had been there since the 1940s. She had doilies on the arms and backs of couch and chairs, and there were knick-knacks on every available space.

Straight across from the fireplace was a door leading to the kitchen. It was compact and neat, with a small table and chairs. Windows, across a closed-in porch, let the sun shine in. From the porch windows I could see a small backyard, with neatly trimmed grass and flowers. The one-car garage stood at the end of the driveway, beside the backyard.

We walked back into the kitchen and to our right, down a small hallway to a bedroom and a small bathroom. The floors were all natural oak, and oak wainscoting went half way up the walls. The bedroom and bath had vintage windows, which brought in light and illuminated the wood floors and wainscoting. I loved this place, but wanted to know about Elmsville.

"I'm from San Diego. I'm a psychotherapist there, but recently divorced and looking for a place to start a new life."

"I understand what you mean. I went through a divorce several years ago, and it wasn't fun. Well, Elmsville is a nice, quiet place to live. And we have a mental hospital just 30 miles from here, near Brookfield."

"Yes, I visited there. In fact, I put in an application to work there."

"Oh, that's good. Lots of people live here and work in Brookfield. And lots of our kids go to college there. People like living here because it's so peaceful. I know you'll like it. And I know you're the one for this house. I could tell the moment I met you."

"Thanks, I just wish I was as sure about it as you are. I love the house, and it's just the right size for me. The trouble is, I don't have much money, until the divorce is final and our house in San Diego sells."

"If it's meant to be, it will be."

"I hope so."

"Visualize what you want, honey. Keep that image in front of you, and it will materialize."

"Thanks, I'll do that. And thank you for showing me the house. I really enjoyed meeting you…and the house."

"My pleasure, see you again."

I drove once more through Elmsville, a typical main street with various stores and an old theatre. A school, a park, police station, fire department, a few restaurants, two gas stations and a few churches spread to the outskirts. I liked the looks of it. I could see myself living here.

What did the lady say? *Visualize what you want and it will materialize.* I thought of how cute the cottage was, how like my grandmother's it was. How perfect it would be for me.

When my grandmother passed away, she willed her possessions to my parents and me. Her furniture came from France, and had a rich mahogany finish. There were crocheted doilies and afghans, and several pieces of pottery, and a set of Havilland dishes, and silverware.

As I drove through the hills and vales back to my beach place, I visualized my grandmother's furniture in the Elmsville cottage. It fit and it looked natural there. As I mentally placed my grandmother's possessions in the little cottage, I suddenly realized I was becoming as obsessed with that little Elmsville cottage as I had been with the MacLean Victorian house.

Back at the beach, I walked along the surf reflecting on its relevance to my life. I had come here to sort things out. I sifted through the experiences in my life, just as the waves wash upon the shore, sifting through the sand, rolling small pebbles over and over until they are round and worn smooth to the touch. My inner being had been worn smooth from the hours of contemplating and relating to this environment and its inhabitants.

I looked up to the house on the cliff. No longer austere, it was bright with activity. I imagined David and Amy painting walls or wallpapering until exhausted, then sitting quietly as David touched up a painting and she worked contentedly on her crafts.

They had two rooms rented out, and Amy's crafts were selling very well. David was giving private painting lessons, and his art was selling at the framing shop in Milton. They were doing just fine.

My interest in the house had brought two young people together in love and creative potential. And it had solved and settled the mystery that had plagued the house for over a century. I wondered if I had not shown interest in it, how long the mystery would have remained.

Another problem I helped to solve was Bryan's situation with Carol and Debby. Bryan told me they had a great time visiting him. He took them up and down the coast from the redwoods to Mexico. He took them to Tijuana, San Diego, Disneyland, Carmel, Monterey and San Francisco.

Bryan received a thank you letter from Debby saying she'd had the best time of her whole life in California. Carol wrote and said essentially the same thing, adding that she and Debby had talked about moving to Milton so Debby could be close to her dad. Bryan said he suspected that Carol wanted this as much as Debby, because he and Carol had hit it off quite well. He knew that I'd be leaving him soon. There were no regrets from either of us. We would always be friends.

There were others, too, whose lives had been altered a bit by my interest in the house. Mother Bernadette and the sisters of the St. James Convent would no longer need to worry about safekeeping the furniture and possessions of Elizabeth MacLean. And Sister Ignatius wouldn't have to keep her secret any longer.

Anna and Harold were two more people whose lives had changed because of my intense curiosity. Their daughter, Amy, was settled in the career she had always wanted, and in love with a wonderful young man. And Anna and Harold had a new interest…an escape from the 9 to 5…where they could keep their minds and bodies active. They looked forward to driving to Milton on the weekends and helping in the restoration project.

Harold helped David redo the gardener's shed into a nursery for Amy. And Anna not only gardened and sewed curtains and slipcovers, but she worked with Amy in developing new recipes for soups, muffins and breads. The house had become a family project.

All of these people, and Sam, Mrs. Erickson, Vivian from the library and Jack from the cemetery all had a lasting effect on my life. I would be somewhat altered by their short entrance into it, as well.

But the one person who would have the most profound effect on me, was the fisherman-philosopher, Tom Smith. I had known from our first meeting that we would become good friends. His dichotomy intrigued me. He was rough, yet cultured. He was rugged, yet educated. And he was gruff, yet sensitive and understanding. He made me realize that there is no black or white to anything. All things are all things. We are made up of all qualities…male-female, hard-soft, analytical-intuitive, strong and sensitive. We are all things. And all things are all things.

We can express whatever we want, however we want to express it, whether through writing, through discussion, through music or art. With a smile or a nod we are constantly expressing and creating.

We can see things, however we choose to see them…through the narrowed-down shutters of self-centeredness, or through an open window of universal consciousness…an awareness of God in all things, creating and expressing all things through us. It is as easy as waking up in the morning, and saying, '*What a beautiful day! Great things are going to happen today!*' We should do this, rather than dragging reluctantly out of bed, and growling at ourselves in the mirror at how awful we look and feel.

As I walked on the beach past the broken-down stairs, which clung futilely to the cliff, I thought about the MacLean sisters, Annabelle and Elizabeth. They lived in their self-imposed isolation, protected on one side by the hedged-in stone structure, and on the other side by the impregnable cliff and its comrade ocean of forcefully pounding waves. This was their sanctuary, away from the whispers and suppositions of humanity.

Possibly, the sisters walked the beach and bared only their feet to the softly rippling waves. Maybe not. Maybe their undeserved guilt kept them chained to the house and its adjacent grounds, to merely approach the edge of the cliff, in order to see the magnificence of the waves rolling in, or watch in obscurity as a ship unloaded its cargo at the dock below.

I could see the gazebo, where Elizabeth watched and waited for her lover to return. Is there something within a person, who is so emotionally involved, that connects them so totally with the other person that they know where they are? And whether they are in this dimension, or the next? Did Elizabeth know her lover was still alive? Or did she just hope? Did the sisters suspect that their father had taken the artist's body out in a boat and thrown it overboard to be eaten by sharks? Maybe this thought added to their guilt.

It is strange that, however contemporary or connected to the rest of the world one might be, such as the sisters seeing ships come in from all parts of the globe, there is something in the mind that can shut the world out so totally.

The mind plays strange tricks on us. It can make us hallucinate or fantasize what people might think of us, resulting in various degrees of paranoia. And it is able to open vistas of awareness through our meditations and dreams. The keynote is to listen. Openness is the only way to understanding. Rather than projecting outwardly, with fears of unmitigated misunderstanding, one must project inwardly, and know that there is goodness within. Above all else, that goodness is infinite and ever expanding, with a compelling need to express itself.

According to Tom, that infinitely expressing and expanding goodness is God. God is the desire within us all to continually create. The Great Creator is continually creating within us, and within everything. It is expressed by us and by everything, in infinite degrees of intelligence, filled with love, and the ultimate creative power.

I walked past the dock, and thought of my many conversations with Tom. Always, I came away knowing more about life, and more about myself. Tom was an expert at making one think. His years as a teacher had honed his qualitative and cognitive capabilities to a fine edge. And he was able to tune that talent into others so carefully, that he enabled them to see with an awareness that illuminated those sensibilities.

This talent came from many years of teaching, but it also was the result of opening to life, and discovering his relationship to it. This awareness didn't come from teaching, or in his wife's death, but in his coming to the beach and communing with its entire atmosphere. Just as with me, this is where my life turned and began to have a new meaning.

I wondered if I would have been as aware of this if I hadn't met Tom. Would this summer have been different if I had spent it here on the beach with no Tom to talk to? Would I have ventured forward and investigated that house, without Tom taunting and teasing me about it? Alone, I might have just passed it off as an interesting old place. But, by talking to Tom about it, my interest kindled into a burning desire to know.

"Nothing is by chance," Tom said, quite matter-of-factly, as he approached me on the beach.

"Huh?!?" I was startled by his remark.

"Us…meeting here. It's not a coincidence. You looked surprised to see me. Why shouldn't I be walking toward your end of the beach, and you toward my end of the beach in our twilight hours?"

"Now, wait a minute! I'm not in my twilight hours, yet!"

"So, you think I am, then?" His eyes held a hint of knowing expectancy, as he teased me into telling the truth.

"I didn't say you were either, Tom. I just refuted that I'm not. You're the English teacher. What does that mean, anyway?"

"Ah ha! You're learning! Do away with the defense, and answer a question with a question. The *twilight hours* is that time of life right before it ends. As in the time of day right before it ends, when the sun is setting and the stars are beginning to flicker on…such as now. That's what I was referring to, little lady…us meeting on the beach at twilight. Why so defensive?"

"Oh, I guess you caught me in a melancholy mood. I only have a couple more weeks here, and was just reminiscing about how things went this summer. As a matter of fact, I was thinking about you, when you appeared in front of me. That's why I looked so surprised. Why did you say that?"

"What?"

"That nothing is by chance."

"Well, it isn't. Do you think it's any accident that the tides roll in and out every day? Or that the sun crosses the sky from east to west without fail? Or do you doubt that that tree up there on the cliff will soon lose its leaves, and look dead for a while, until new leaves come forth? No. You know these truths to be self-evident. You can depend on the earthly cycles. Why not the consistency of our lives?"

"What do you mean?"

"You're always asking that question." He scoffed and scowled at me.

"Because, I don't understand everything you say. Or if I think I understand it, I'm not always sure how you mean it."

"That's all right, Laura. I was just teasing you again. You should know by now to take only half of what I say seriously." Tom smiled, with a twinkle in his eye.

"But, the question is, Tom," I said so profoundly, "which half is the truth."

"Good question. But you'll have to figure that one out on your own. To know is to do, but to do is not always to know."

Once again, I felt as though I were sparring with the Cheshire cat.

"That's one I'm really going to have to think about, Tom. But it's getting cold. Let's go somewhere to talk."

"Good! It's time you visited my place. That's what I was up to. I was coming to invite you to a home-cooked fish dinner."

"So, you finally caught some fish?" I asked excitedly.

"Yes, at the market. But we can pretend this is a culmination of our futile efforts at fishing. Besides, I personally feel that fish taste better if you don't have to gut them."

We laughed and sauntered along the beach, as little flickering fireflies gradually became brightly lit beach homes.

Tom's home was painted a soft shade of blue. As we stepped onto a broad deck, which had matching blue and white furniture, I remarked, "Blue and white, huh? These colors are very symbolic of truth and spiritual awareness. They are significant to your way of life, Tom."

"That may be true, but they were also significantly cheaper than any others I saw." Tom was teasing me again, with his altruistic attitude about my analyzing everything.

Undaunted, I retaliated with his own words. "Nothing is by chance, Tom."

He gave me a wrinkled grin and growled, "Just because you're so smart, little lady, I'm going to let you make the salad. Just dig through that fridge, and bring out everything you can find, and throw it into a bowl. The more the better, when it comes to salad."

"The more the better, when it comes to life, too," I smirked.

"Jesus, Laura, you *have* learned a lot! I'll have to call you my star pupil."

"Thanks to you, Tom, I *have* learned a lot this summer. In fact, that's what I was thinking about when I met you on the beach. I was wondering if I hadn't met you, if I'd have ever investigated that old house. And David and Amy wouldn't have met, nor would Amy have found out about her ancestors, nor would Anna and Harold have found something to bring new interest into their lives."

"Wow, that's a big responsibility for one little lady's shoulders. But, don't act so smug about it. If you hadn't done it, someone else would have. It's as simple as that. It was something that needed to be done. It would get done somehow, with or without you."

"Oh, Tom, you always find a way to burst my balloon. I was really feeling good about helping all of those people. Now you say that anyone could have done it. That's deflating."

"It is meant to be. Why should you feel so smug about helping all of those people? It wasn't you that did it. It was the universal creative energy that we call God, working through you. You're going off on an ego trip, doc. You know better than that."

"Darn! You got me again, Tom. You're right. I was on an ego trip. I can see what you meant, now. Nothing is by chance. I was just the instrument by which God worked. It all would have fallen into place without me. Someone else would have picked up the vibrations and gone with the idea, if I hadn't," I said complacently, as I pulled a head of lettuce apart.

Tom was beating a batter of tempura for the fish fillets. "I didn't do that to deflate your ego, Laura. I wanted you to stop thinking about how everything around you has changed, and start realizing how *you* have changed. How has all of this affected you? How are you different from that girl I first met on the dock?"

God, he was sagacious. I felt as if he could see right through me. "Okay, when we met, I was still upset about the divorce. I was still going through the various stages of loss – denial, remorse, guilt, regret, and anger. I think I was feeling all of these things at the same time… just shifting from one to the other. Talking to you, and getting involved with that house and the people surrounding it, changed me. I got out of myself, and started being concerned about others. Maybe that's the key to self-awareness. It comes through helping others."

"You are enlightened, young lady." Tom dipped the fillets into the batter, and dropped them into the hot oil. They immediately puffed up into light, crispy morsels, which looked as though they would melt in your mouth.

"You like dealing with metaphors and symbolisms," he continued. "Think of yourself as this fish fillet." He poked his fork at a raw fish fillet in the dish. "You lie in the dish, cold and soggy, heavily soaking in your juices. You would remain there, in that condition, unless some force came along and lifted you out of where you are, and gave you new life, through a new perspective. So, I picked you up, and plunked you into a new way of thinking," he plunked the fillet into the batter.

"But," he continued, as he rolled the fillet in the batter, "you aren't worth a damn just lying there sloshing around with those new concepts. You have to take yourself out, into the world, and apply what you've been taught." He stabbed the battered fillet, and dropped it into the sizzling oil. It immediately puffed up and floated to the top.

"You see? Once you become involved with your environment, there is no way you'll remain the same. You emulate enlightenment. Just as that heavy hunk of fish changes appearance and rises to the top of the oil, you take on a new look and become lighter. It's a dichotomy, Laura, the more you take on, the lighter you become."

"Wow! That's interesting. I never thought of it that way." I watched the fillets bobbing in the oil, like little lifeboats bouncing upon a bubbly sea.

I set the table and we sat with white wine, salad, bread and the best fish I'd ever had. Tom claimed it was the beer he added to the batter that made it so light.

While we ate, I told Tom about the remodeling project Amy, David, Anna and Harold were doing. I also told him about Bryan's rediscovering Carol.

"Good!" Tom scoffed. "He wasn't right for you."

"How did you know?"

"Anyone who would take a pretty girl like you to San Francisco, and bring her back the same day, has a few screws loose. I knew you wouldn't go for him."

"Wait a minute, Tom. Don't you think I had anything to say about it? I didn't want to stay in San Francisco. That's why we didn't stay," I said indignantly.

"Well, if you'd have been with me, and I was 30 years younger, you would have wanted to stay." Tom said this with serious conviction.

"I don't doubt that for a minute, Tom." I smiled back at him. Then I got up and started clearing the table.

"Wait a minute. You're not going to wash my dishes," Tom growled.

"Why not?" I asked, as I scraped the scraps off our plates.

"Because I have all of tomorrow to do them. Besides, I have some books I want to show you. Come on."

He led me into the living room. The furniture there was conservative and comfortable. The contemporary style furnishings went well with the high-pitched, open framed ceiling, and the massive windows, which looked out to the sea. A balcony hung above the living room.

"There are two bedrooms and a bath upstairs. And down here there's a bedroom and a bathroom. But I converted the downstairs bedroom into a study." He led the way into a room with a desk, a couch, a lamp table and two full walls of books.

"Wow, You *do* have a lot of books!"

"Oh, I gave most of them away to the school library when I retired. These are the ones I like to reread. Mostly the classics, but many of them are new. I bought them while I've been hibernating at the beach.

These are the ones I'd like you to read." He pointed to several shelves containing books by Richard Bach, Wayne Dyer, Gerald Jampolsky, Marianne Williamson, Harmon Bro, Gina Cerminara, Esther Hicks, Hugh Lynn Cayce, Khalil Gibran, Mother Teresa, the Dalai Lama, Martin Luther King, Jr., and others.

"Oh, Tom, I'm going to be leaving in a couple of weeks. I wish you'd have loaned me the books earlier in the summer."

"I wasn't sure you were ready for them. There was a lot of contention in you at that time. You needed to come out of yourself before you could open up to these concepts."

"Yes, I see what you mean."

"So, where are you going? Back to San Diego?"

"No, Tom, I don't think so. I've fallen in love with this area. I like San Diego, but lots of unhappy memories there. And...that was a different person who lived and worked there. This new person wants to be in a new environment and start from scratch. I discovered this summer, that wherever I go, I will make friends and have lasting relationships. Just as I have done here at the beach."

"I know you've been driving around looking. Have you found anything?"

"I think so. I filled out an application at the Northern Counties State Mental Hospital near Brookfield. It's about an hours drive from here. I like that area, tucked between the hills and valleys of the wine country. Everything is so green there. And the sky is so blue and clear. I even found a little house I like."

"Really? In Brookfield?" Tom sat down in his desk chair. I slumped down onto the couch.

"No, not Brookfield, but Elmsville, a small town about 30 miles from Brookfield. The hospital is between them. There is a quaint little cottage there, which reminds me of the cottage my grandfather built, in San Clemente, in the 1940s for my grandmother. It has one bedroom and a bath, and is small and cozy."

"Are you going to buy it?"

"I don't know. The woman was anxious to sell, because she needs to move to her ailing sister's place in Monterey."

"Have you looked at any other places?"

"No, just this one. It caught my eye. And, even though I wasn't thinking of living in that town, I just wanted to see inside of that house."

"Aha! And you did, and you fell in love with it."

"Right. I guess I did fall in love with it, because, even though I wasn't so sure about it when I drove away, I headed toward town to look around. Then all the way back here I thought about it, and visualized my furniture in that little cottage."

"Then it is the house for you."

"Why do you say that?" I wondered why he always said everything with such conviction.

"Because, little lady, you were drawn to that house by a power that is beyond any reasoning on your part…just as you were drawn to the house on the cliff. It is meant to be, or you wouldn't have been drawn toward it. So, what are you going to do about it?"

"Oh, I'll go out looking around for some more places to live."

"You've already found a place to live." Tom smiled at me, with raised eyebrows.

"You mean that little cottage? Oh, it will probably be snatched up before I can put together a financial plan."

"Not if it is meant for you, Laura. It will still be there."

As I carried an armload of books back to my beach house, I thought about what Tom had said. The more I thought about it, the more feasible the idea seemed. I began visualizing myself in that little house. I knew I would get enough in the divorce settlement…half of the sale of our house in San Diego…to buy a small place for myself. But that wouldn't come for a while. And I had been assured of the job at

Northern Counties Mental Hospital. So, there was one other option. I would phone my parents in the morning.

I fell asleep reading a line from one of Tom's books. *What you can conceive, and believe, you can achieve.*

At 10 am, I had a phone call from the administrator of the Northern Counties Mental Hospital asking if I had decided on the job. He said I could start as soon as I wanted. We agreed I would come in and sign a contract that afternoon. I was amazed and excited that this would happen so soon. I was reminded of what I had read before falling asleep... *What you can conceive, and believe, you can achieve.*

I had been keeping in touch with my parents in San Diego, and telling them about the Victorian house, and the various friends I had met here. Now it was time to phone them and break the news.

"Mother, I have found a small house up here that I want to buy. It's just like the one Grandfather Christopher built for grandmother. I can just see her furniture in it."

"Oh, that is nice, dear. But I wish it weren't so far away."

"It's only an hour and a half flight, and it's just eight hours by car. I'll come to see you often."

"That's good. But what about your work?"

"I have applied at Northern Counties State Mental Hospital in Brookfield. They want me, and I'll sign a contract with them today."

"Brookfield, is that where you'll be living?"

"No. The house is in Elmsville, which is 30 miles from Brookfield. It is a very quiet, peaceful, small community. It's just what I want now... less traffic and commotion."

"That sounds nice. But we will miss you."

"I'll miss you, too. But, as I said, I'll come to see you often."

"Is there anything we can do to help you?"

"Yes, Mother, there is. I'm virtually broke, until the house down there is sold. Could you help me with the down payment? Then I'll be able to handle the payments with my salary from the hospital. And I'll pay you back as soon as I can."

"Of course we'll help. And don't worry about paying us back. It's your inheritance, anyway."

"Thanks, Mother. I'll have to get back to you about how much."

"Okay, and we'll wire you the money."

I was relieved, even though I knew they had the money, and would gladly give it to me. Just having it settled brought a sense of completion.

Now I looked forward to driving to Brookfield for the interview, and to Elmsville to see the cottage again. I hadn't taken the phone number down, because I really hadn't a clue that I'd want to buy the house. But when I got there, the sign was still up...*For Sale By Owner.*

Tom was right – nothing is by chance.

Chapter 16

The Wedding

It had been several months since I had moved to Elmsville. I visited the beach a few times to see Tom, and to see how the Victorian house renovation was coming along. Then things got hectic at work, and I didn't get back for a while.

When the wedding invitation came, I was so elated. It was as if everything had culminated into the final chapter. The story was ended, and the house was content, as were David, Amy and her parents.

Driving toward Milton, I anticipated seeing Amy and David again. I knew the house would be in a blissful state, with the excitement of their wedding preparations.

As I drove down the lane by the magnificent homes on the cliff, my eagerness heightened. When I saw the house, my heart leaped, as if seeing an old friend after a long absence. It looked wonderful. Newly painted white, it looked even bigger than it had before. The hedge was neatly trimmed, and a sign stood beside it:

THE MACLEAN HOUSE BED & BREAKFAST, & TEA ROOM - "WELCOME"

A small sign hanging under it: *AMY'S ART, ANTIQUES & NURSERY.* An arrow pointed toward the gardener's house, with the word *"PARKING"*. A young man motioned for me to enter there.

The hedge had been opened up where the road to the carriage house had previously been. Now, a new road led past Amy's Art, Antiques & Nursery, and to the newly built carriage house, with ample parking in front of both. I parked among the other cars, and followed the path alongside of the house toward the front. The path was marked by white bows and ribbons, draped from post to post, along a profusion of azaleas, hydrangeas, hibiscus and rose bushes. The whole house was surrounded in the glorious color of flowering plants.

I walked up the steps to the open front door. The porch and entryway were decorated with potted plants and hanging baskets. Upon entering, I was pleasantly surprised at the formality of the scene. People stood around in lovely, light, summer colors, chattering and laughing in gay tonality.

Looking to my right, I could see into the parlor. David's painting of Amy in the gazebo hung above the fireplace. Two majestic candlesticks stood on either side of it. The furniture was arranged around the room just as it must have been a century ago. But, on small side-tables and bookshelves were placed David's miniatures of the house, the gazebo, the carriage house, the nursery, the gardens, and some ocean views. There were also a few of Amy's smaller craft items here for sale.

I walked to my left past some people I didn't know, and into the large ballroom. The shiny hardwood floor was dotted with round tables and chairs, with white tablecloths and flower arrangements. People were standing in groups around and between the tables.

Above the fireplaces hung the portraits of Annabelle and Elizabeth MacLean.

"They look good there, don't they?"

I turned around and Mother Bernadette and Sister Ignatius stood beside me.

"Yes, they do. I'm so happy for them, and for Amy and David."

"We are too," said Mother Bernadette. "They have been coming to church in town. So we see them often. They are so sweet. And they've done wonders with this house. I'm sure Annabelle and Elizabeth are very happy now."

"Yes, I was just thinking the same thing. And the furniture looks good here too."

"Yes. We were happy to give it back to them. They have a lot of good plans for this place," said Sister Bernadette.

"They certainly do. And they have the energy and talent to do it."

"I'm sure they will be very successful," said Sister Ignatius.

"They will be successful in all that they do, because they have such great faith in each other," I said.

"Yes. Faith is the key to success," said Sister Ignatius.

Then I saw Vivian Hendricks, the curator of the Milton Museum. She smiled and walked up to me.

"Hi, Laura. Isn't this wonderful?"

"Hi, Vivian. Yes, it certainly is. Do you know Mother Bernadette and Sister Ignatius?"

"Hi, yes, I know Mother Bernadette, but not Sister Ignatius."

"Sister Mary Angelica passed the MacLean family information on to Sister Ignatius, who shared it with Bryan and me."

"Oh, yes, you told me about that. And, Sister, you lived here with Sister Mary Angelica?"

"Yes, I did. But that was decades ago."

"I guess it has changed quite a bit since then," said Vivian.

"Yes, it has. When the convent inherited it, the gardens were almost dead. The MacLean sisters couldn't keep it up. We brought it back to life. I loved working here in the gardens."

"Then," I added, "as various families lived here and left, it became decrepit again. I'm so glad Amy and David bought it. The house and grounds are just beautiful."

"Yes!" They agreed.

Then Vivian said to me, "David and Amy and her folks have done wonders with this place. Do you recognize some of this furniture from the convent and from our museum?"

"Yes. It was so nice of you to give the kids the MacLean furniture."

"Well, they offered to buy it from us, but I knew they really couldn't afford it with all of the work they were doing here, and I wanted it to be back in its rightful place here in this house. We have other nineteenth century furniture to display."

"That's good. I know the kids really appreciate it."

"Yes, they are such sweet kids. I'm so happy for them."

"Me too. Oh, there's Bryan Lewis. Excuse me Vivian…Sisters." I walked over to Bryan and his wife and daughter.

"Well, I wondered when you'd get here," Bryan smiled at me. "Laura, I want you to meet my wife, Carol, and our daughter Debby."

I put out my hand. "Hi, Carol, I'm so happy to finally meet you, and delighted to hear of your marriage." We shook hands.

"Thanks, Laura. We were married in Chicago, because our families are there. I'm glad to meet you, too. Bryan has told me so much about you, and this house. It's a wonderful thing you did for Amy and David."

"I loved solving the mystery of the house. I'm just glad it had a happy ending."

"Yes, this is a beautiful ending, isn't it?"

"Yes, it is." I turned to Debby. "Hi Debby. How do you like Milton?"

"Oh, I think it's great!"

"Do you miss the big city activity in Chicago?"

"No, not really. It's quieter here, and more peaceful. I've always wanted to live near the ocean."

"Have you made friends here?"

"Yeah, we just moved here at the end of school. But, I've met some friends in the neighborhood, and kids of people dad knows. They're real nice."

"That's good. I've found this area to be kind of laid back and easy going, not like the pressure and anxiety of the big cities."

"We like that too," said Carol as she put her arm around Bryan and squeezed him.

He smiled and said, "Yeah."

"I'm so happy for you." I smiled at all three of them, then excused myself. "Now I must try to find the mother and father of the bride."

I saw Harold first. I walked up to him and shook his hand. "Congratulations Harold!"

He looked surprised to see me. "Well, Hello, Laura. Yeah, I guess congratulations *are* in order. Nowadays you never know if they'll get married or not."

"Now, Harold." Anna walked up. "You know they told us from the beginning that they'd be married in June." Then she hugged me. "Laura, it's so good to see you. It's been a long time."

"I know. Too long! It's good seeing you again, too. I didn't realize how much I missed you and this house, until I got here."

"Well, you're just going to have to come back more often."

"I will. And you must see my little house. When are you two going to visit me in Elmsville?"

"Well, now that the house is finished we can use our weekends to do some sightseeing. Right, Harold?"

"Right! And you'll be the first person we'll visit, Laura."

"Good! I'll hold you to that. Elmsville is a very nice, quiet, little town. A good place to retire to," I hinted.

"That's something we've talked about, Laura, being closer to the kids. We'll probably take some trips up here and look around."

At that moment a gruff voice from behind me said, "Well, you finally escaped that lilliputian valley of yours, huh, little lady?"

I turned around and gave Tom a big bear hug and kissed him on the cheek.

"Hey," he said. "You'd better watch out. My fiancé might get jealous!" He stepped back, and I saw Mrs. Erickson standing beside him.

"Tom! Really? I can't believe this. Is it true?" I hugged Mrs. Erickson. I didn't want to call her Mrs. Erickson, now, but didn't know her first name.

"Yes, Betty and I are going to be married here, too," Tom answered. "David and Amy, enterprising kids that they are, want to offer the house for weddings now. But they had to have theirs here first, as sort of a christening. So we've been waiting for this day."

"Oh, Tom," Betty grinned, "You only asked me few weeks ago."

"Well, I would have whisked you off to Reno, if you hadn't wanted to be married in this damn house." We all laughed.

"So, how did you two meet?" I looked from one to the other.

"Well," Tom began, "after you left, Laura, I got lonely. No one to fish with. And I got curious about this house. It seemed to be my only link with you. So I came up here to visit with David and Amy. And I met Betty. She's been roaming around here ever since her son went away to college."

"And," Betty interjected, "we discovered that we have a lot of the same interests. We have some of the same books, and we both like to travel, though I didn't travel much until I met Tom."

"Right. We've taken a lot of excursions up and down the coast this year. And we're going to Europe for our honeymoon." Tom smiled fondly at Betty. She looked lovingly into his eyes.

"Have you set a date? I want to be here for it."

"Yes, Laura," Betty answered. "We just decided a couple of days ago. That's why you haven't gotten a card yet."

"Right," said Tom. "We're going to run this place for the kids, while they take a week's honeymoon trip to Mexico. Amy wants to bring some pots back to sell. Then a couple of weeks after that, we'll get married. Our trip to Europe begins in July."

"That's wonderful! I'm so happy for you!" I hugged them again.

Then someone announced that it was time for the ceremony and we were to go through the French doors to the backyard. We walked the pathway through gardens of roses, iris, begonias, tulips, daisies, morning glories and much more.

The green lawn in front of the gazebo was set with rows of white chairs. At the beginning of each row were white posts with blue and lavender bows, and small baskets of flowers.

We sat facing the gazebo. It looked so pretty, glistening white in the sunlight. Purple wisteria wound its way through the lattice slats of the ceiling, as pansies and impatiens bordered its bottom edge.

I looked to the cliff and was surprised to see a white, wooden fence along it, with a gate leading to a new stairway to the beach. The work that David and Amy had done was impressive. It was exhilarating to be able to share this beauty.

Amy wore a long, white Victorian style gown, with a lace veil flowing behind her. David and his best man and ushers wore late 19th century tuxedos. Amy's bridesmaids wore lavender satin. And her little flower girl and ring bearer were her brother's children.

They all stood in the gazebo as the priest performed the ceremony. I wept tears of joy. Betty, who sat beside me, cried too. I imagined that she felt as I did, that this was the completion of Elizabeth's long vigil. Now her spirit would be at peace, and it could go on to do, whatever spirits do, when they have satisfied their souls.

As one book ends, another one begins.

NEXT IN THE SERIES:

THE DREAM ANALYST AND THE TEACHER

CPSIA information can be obtained
at www.ICGtesting.com
Printed in the USA
FSOW01n0407311017
40410FS

9 781946 005052